Lock Down Publications and Ca$h
Presents

Killaz On Standby

Nature of the Beast

Written By

IRA B.

First Edition 2025

Printed in the United States of America

This is a work of fiction. Names, characters, places, and incidents either are products of the author's imagination or are used fictitiously. Any similarity to actual events or locales or persons, living or dead, is entirely coincidental.

Lock Down Publications
P.O. Box 944
Stockbridge, GA 30281
www.lockdownpublications.com

Like our page on Facebook: Lock Down Publications
www.facebook.com/lockdownpublications.ldp

Stay Connected with Us!

Text **LOCKDOWN** to 22828 to stay up-to-date with new releases, sneak peaks, contests and more…

Like our page on Facebook:
Lock Down Publications

Join Lock Down Publications/The New Era Reading Group

Visit our website:
www.lockdownpublications.com

Follow us on Instagram:
Lock Down Publications

Email Us: We want to hear from you!

PROLOGUE

Naomi was deep in her thoughts as she stood before the kitchen sink, polishing off the rest of the dishes. Her heart conflicted with her thoughts and how she was feeling at that present moment. Those very thoughts had something to do with the man she'd loved and cared about for as long as she could remember. Thoughts of Roland Scott, the father of her children, the one who had caused her heart both pain and love for so long.

After spending the past ten years in federal prison for tax evasion, drug charges, and conspiracy, Roland was released two months ago. And for those two months, all he cared about was spending time with his three daughters and being the father to them that he never got the chance to be. They were eleven years old now, a trio of beautiful triplets: Joya, Moya, and Toya. They were the link that would forever bind them together, no matter how much Naomi believed her and Roland's relationship would never be the same as it once was.

He went in a gangsta, and he damn sure emerged a gangsta, a mentality that she no longer desired to entertain again. She was done with street niggas. But her love for Roland was strong; he had been there for her through thick and thin.

Suddenly the sound of the front door opening alerted Naomi that her girls had finally returned. The house immediately exploded with joyous noise and activity. She stepped towards the kitchen doorway and saw that they all were loaded with shopping bags. Roland looked up at her with a sheepish grin on his face. Once again, he had accomplished another special moment out with the girls. They had gone out for dinner and a movie, but somehow they found shopping to go along with the occasion. Naomi stepped into the living room and was instantly attacked by one of her daughters with a big bear hug.

"Look what I got!" said Joya. This was the most predictable one, Joya. It was probably her idea that Roland took them on another shopping spree, because Joya was always asking for money to buy new things.

"Me too, ma!" said Toya, the scholar of the crew, the one who was very intellectual and humble. "Look what I got too!"

"Whatcha got?" Naomi replied with curiosity. She took a seat on the bigger sofa. First, Joya showed off the new Dior sweater and female Air Jordans that her father had bought for her, along with other things. Then Toya revealed her new MacPad tablet computer, a hat, some pink Fendi shades, and a bead bracelet. When Naomi turned to Moya she was busy programming her iPhone.

"You got a new cellphone?"

"Yep." Moya looked up at her and said humbly.

"What else you get?"

Naomi was told by her daughter that a new phone was all she really wanted. When Naomi looked up at Roland, he just shrugged and nodded in response. That was so like Moya— she didn't ask for much; her independence was noteworthy. At her age, she believed in earning her keep, hustling to get what she wanted, rather than always having her hand out. She was more like Roland than the other two, and Naomi knew that one day Moya was going to rule wherever she decided to go in life.

"I got something for you too, Naomi," Roland finally spoke up from where had been perched on the arm of the black leather recliner chair.

5

Right at that moment, Moya set her new cellphone aside and grinned up at her mother. Both Joya and Toya started giggling like they found something funny.

"What's so damn funny?" Naomi replied as she watched Roland make his way over to her.

"I love you with all my heart, Naomi. You gave me the best thang a man could ever ask for. And now I want to give you the best thang a wife could ever ask for in her husband," said Roland.

Naomi felt her heart skip a beat.

He got down on one knee and took her left hand into his possession. With his other hand, Roland produced a 7-carat diamond ring with a platinum band from the pocket of his Kapital jeans. When Naomi laid eyes on the ring and a flood of emotions washed over her. She became so speechless that no words came out of her mouth.

"Will you marry me?"

Tears welled up in Naomi's eyes.

"Say yes, mama!" Joya blurted out loud.

"Say yes! You know you want to." Moya moved over closer to her parents and laid a hand upon Roland's muscular shoulder. "Remember when you told us that Daddy was the only man for you?"

"She said that?" Roland regarded his daughter with astonishment, then turned his gaze back up at the woman he was promising his life to.

Before another word was spoken, the front door of the house was kicked in. Then three armed goons with ski masks entered with heavy artillery. At once, Roland bolted to his feet only to get bashed in the face by the stock of one of the goon's assault rifle.

Toya screamed bloody murder.

"Where that money and dope at, muthafucka?" said the goon who attacked Roland.

Without hesitation, Roland told him he had a couple thousand in his pocket and more money in his BMW outside. But that only caused him to be bashed in the face again with the goon's weapon.

"I don't want no petty change, nigga! I know you boss status—where that shit at!"

"I told you. I'm not in the game no more."

He hit Roland again.

Right at that moment Moya had seen enough and rushed over to attack the gunman that was harming her father. Moya pushed and kicked him in the leg, only to get backhanded so hard across the face she flew across the room.

"Why you doing this?" Naomi cried, having gathered both Joya and Toya protectively in her arms. She wanted to go for Moya but was afraid to move.

"I got somethin' that'll get your mind right." The goon nodded at one of his men and told them to make an example out of Moya.

Roland and Naomi watched in horror as the other masked goon grabbed ahold of Moya and held her down on the floor. Then he took out a pistol from his waistline and pressed it into Moya's hand against the floor. Moya swung a fist up at him and clocked him across the right side of his jaw.

"Do it, nigga!" the lead goon ordered.

Blocka!

At the deafening blast of the gun, Moya cried out in a blood-curdling scream that sent Roland into a whole 'nother state of mind. Roland bolted from the chair and landed a vicious blow to the face of the man. Then another blast rang out from the pump-action shotgun from the third goon standing by the blast hit Roland dead center of his broad chest. Then the lead goon shot him twice more before they ran for the door and got ghost.

Moya, who was crying and going into shock from her wound, fought against the pain and crawled across the floor towards her father. She was a tough little cookie, and her life from that point forward was written in stone. Seeing her father die was a very shocking reality. Naomi couldn't believe her eyes; her heart was broken once again. She was so close to reaching that pinnacle of happiness, and now it was taken away. But when it rains it pours, and all one could do was pray for no more rain.

Chapter 1
Ten Years Later—

Moya was snoring lightly on her queen-sized bed when she felt herself being awakened by a constant nudging against her arm. When she finally woke up, she turned over to see one of the few most trusted niggas in her life. One look into Monster's golden eyes and she already knew what time it was. Moya got up and tossed her thick, shapely legs over the side of the bed.

"What's up, my nigga!" Moya stroked the head of Monster, which was a big tank of a dog, a German Rottweiler, and just as vicious as Moya herself.

After reaching for the half-blunt of runtz weed on the ashtray upon the nightstand, Moya put fire to it and got up from the bed. Obviously, Monster was hungry, so she led him into the kitchen of her condominium apartment in downtown Tallahassee. While Monster fed his face Moya entered the spacious expensive furnished living room, where she switched on her large 70-inch Sony flatscreen TV mounted on the far wall. She then switched it to the channel 6 WCTV News, where the latest top stories were showing.

". . . where I'm standing here on Lake Branford Road of south Tallahassee, where just up the street here, TPD is still

9

at the scene of a possible double homicide. According to authorities, a call was reported of shots being fired within the First Elizabeth Baptist Church, where upon arrival authorities found the owner of the church, Reverend Harold Banks, and another unidentified victim dead by gunshot wounds to the head and torso. No further witnesses have been confirmed yet, but authorities believe the deaths were caused by an act of robbery . . ."

That was as far as Moya went with watching the TV before she reached for her iPhone 12 lying on the coffee table in front of her. She called the number that she had been anticipating since the night before.

"Good morning, Moya," answered a deep tenor's voice.

"Good morning. How's your cup of coffee this morning?" she replied with a look of earnestness.

"It's rich and very tasty."

"How rich?"

"A quarter million dollars rich," he said.

Moya smiled. "Good day. Thank you," she replied.

"You're welcome."

When Monster entered the room with his thick gold Cuban link chain swinging around his equally thick neck, Moya kissed him on the head and mushed him in the face. He then head-butted her in the leg and dodged her right hook to his jaw before they began wrestling. This was something like a morning ritual for them. Moya was excited about the successful hit she had taken and was now 250,000 dollars richer.

To her, the hit was just another play in the game of life.

Moya the steppa. She was nothing to be fucked up with. She and her team of youngins were vicious, thorough, and making a lot of noise in the street. They were a force to be reckoned with, and by any means necessary, they was gonna get it how they live.

After playing with Monster for a while, Moya hopped in the shower to get ready for her day. The life of a gangstress was in demand. She supplied what they needed.

***

As always, the sight of her students made her heart swell with love and pride.

Toya stood at the door of her classroom and watched as her fourth-grade homeroom class trickled into the room one after the other. For nearly four months now, since the class's primary homeroom teacher, Mrs. Cynthia Jacobs, was out on maternity leave, Toya became the substitute teacher and was loving every moment of it. And her students adored her like crazy, especially seeing that she was young and hip, unlike Mrs. Jacobs who was in her early forties and knowing damn well she had waited nearly too late to bear a child. The woman damn near lost her life giving birth to her son.

Toya interacted with each one of her students as they filed into the room. Some she admired immensely; some she thought were too adorable, and a few of them worked her nerves, but there was some that concerned her to the core. Toya loved her babies; she was crazy about kids, same as her twin Moya, who would go to the ends of the earth to see that they are cared for.

11

"How was everybody's weekend?" Toya asked once everybody was in the room and settled. A chorus of responses erupted throughout the room from her students. She smiled at some of their responses, and some she caught in the midst caused her only to shake her head.

A minute later, the classroom door opened and in walked Desiree Smith, whom Tonya considered the prettiest and most adorable child in the school. Toya thought she had the most beautiful set of hazel brown eyes. She made the room glow with her smile. But today those same beautiful brown eyes were dark and sad-looking, as she dragged herself over to her assigned desk.

"Good morning, Desiree," said Toya.

"Hey." Desiree seemed to have struggled just to get that one word out. To Toya, she appeared as though she was in pain. The girl slid into her desk and two other little girls behind her picked fun at her dirty shoes. Toya told them to cut it out, then regarded Desiree with an apologetic glance, but Desiree paid her no mind at all.

"Okay," Toya let out a deep sigh. "Today we're gonna start with simple multiplication. Everybody take out your charts and calculator," she announced.

While in the process of sharpening her student's math skills, Toya couldn't help but observe Desiree's behavior, which made her suspicious, and Desiree was pretending as though nothing about her actions was worthy of concern. The girl was hurting and it was obvious by the agonizing expression on her face every time she moved.

When it came down to the well-being and feelings of her students, Toya was always there to assist them in whatever it took to bring them comfort.

She was loyal to her job as a teacher and dedicated beyond measure to her students. That very moment was no different from any other moment where her devotion to care for her babies was needed.

"Dez," Toya called out to Desiree when first period bell rang and concluded their time. Desiree looked up at her, and Toya beckoned her over with a wave. Meanwhile, the rest of the students were heading out the door to their next class.

Desiree, who had been slow to get up, gathered up the courage to approach her teacher's desk without giving up the fact that she was in great discomfort.

"Yes, ma'am," Desiree said in the softest voice.

"What's wrong, baby girl?" Toya reached out to touch her arm, and the girl flinched.

"I'm okay, Ms. Scott. I just got a tummy ache, that's all," replied Desiree. But Toya wasn't convinced; she knew a lie when she saw one, and Desiree was telling a bold-faced lie.

"Just a tummyache, that's it?"

The girl nodded.

Reluctantly, Toya sighed and nodded, then she advised Desiree to see the school's clinical nurse if her stomach worsened. She promised she would and tried to hurry along to her next class. With the shake of her head, Toya could only hope that Desiree's discomfort didn't have anything to do with abuse in the physical sense. Although it was an elementary school, it still had its share of violence, and Toya had had to put a stop to plenty of bullying.

The Desiree that she knew didn't get bullied; she was one of the feisty ones, very clever and lonesome. She took up for her friends, which were only two at most, whose names were Samuel and Alexis. So to see her getting pushed around at school was the last thing Toya would expect from the young girl.

Unless her pain resulted from home . . . but Toya very much doubted Desiree was being treated so unfairly.

Sometimes you just never know.

Life is cold.

A little after noon that very same day, Joya entered through the front door of the apartment that she shared with Toya. Stepping in after her was her boyfriend, Zamon, palming her bubble booty in the process. The way her 40-inch ass bounced and jiggled in her Autumn Adeigbo Camille dress was a sight to see. It had its own performance, and Zamon couldn't help but grip them cheeks.

The second the front door closed shut, Joya attacked his pants zipper and freed his manhood. She lazily licked the length of his tool and spat on the head. Joya gave the dick a couple of customary strokes to spread the saliva all over it. Then she got down to business and swallowed every inch of him without a gag reflex. Zamon grabbed her by the back of the head and fucked her mouth with long strokes of pure pleasure. After a couple minutes of mouth service, Joya jumped to her feet and lifted the back of her dress up over her thick hips.

"You know how I want it, baby. I need to feel you inside of me," Joya said sensually, reaching back to guide Zamon deep inside her asshole.

"Shit!" Zamon gripped her waist with one hand and took ahold of her shoulder. He plunged in and out of her ass like a porn star video.

"Stop bullshittin' and dip in that shit, bae!" Joya said, looking back over her shoulder.

This was her way of life—the power of the pussy—and her sex game was on point. Joya sold sex to get her money bag up; she blackmailed and manipulated her way into the money. From doctors to lawyers and college professors to drug dealers, Joya was in all of their pockets, and she was damn good at it. Joya played her hand so close that Zamon was oblivious to what was going on. But she took good care of her man, made sure he was laced in the best fashion labels, and kept his pockets fat. To Zamon, he knew he had caught himself a diamond, but little did he know how wrong he was.

Despite her sex games and mind games, Joya was finishing up her senior year in college. She attended FAMU College on an academic scholarship, majoring in Music Education and having the time of her life. She was quite intelligent—one of the smartest in her class. Toya was ambitious and would not let nothing get in the way of her goals.

When Joya felt Zamon's dick twitching inside of her ass and knew he was on the verge of cumming, she pushed away from him and dropped to her knees. She took his dick deep into her throat, and Zamon gripped her head, forcing her to stay on the dick and swallow every drop of his semen.

"Damn." Zamon's legs were shaking.

"Damn what, hoe?" She wiped her mouth clean.

"You a freak!"

She laughed. "And you love every bit of it too." Joya reclaimed her clutch purse and backpack from the floor of the foyer. She then made her way to her bedroom while Zamon lounged on the living room sofa and flipped the TV to ESPN Sports. Their little fuck session had worn him out and he needed to recharge.

Back in her bedroom, Joya removed her blue dress and laid it across the bed. Then she reached into the side compartment of her backpack for the thick white envelope she had there. She opened the envelope and thumbed through the Benjamin Franklins with silent triumph.

"All about the Benjamins, baby!" sang Joya after extracting ten bills from the stack and storing the rest inside her closet safe. She would give Zamon the grand to put in his pocket.

Today she had conned one of her victims out of fifty thousand dollars. He was a married business owner who had a thing for young Black girls. Although Joya, as well as her sisters, reminded you of a younger version of Alicia keys, her youthfulness and performances in her con games were what kept her prey in line. Today, she made the business owner see the error of his ways, and he had no choice but to pay up.

Scheming on some paper was the norm for her.

Today was a good day.

Life was good.

And the pussy was still powerful.

Chapter 2

A bottle of Hennessy and a blunt of that gas was all Moya needed to get her day started. Moya checked the time on her $14,500 Cartier Ballon Bleu watch and poured some liquor in her red Solo cup. She was riding shotgun in her black-on-black Mustang Dark Horse while her right-hand man Tito whipped it through the city streets. He couldn't wait to push her new car, and Tito was pushing it like it was his shit. This was the closest nigga to Moya besides her team of youngins. Tito was the truth; he was loyal, and Moya loved that nigga. Together they had wreaked havoc in the streets of Tallahassee and all its surrounding areas. From bustin' heads to their murder game, and even lockin' shit down in the dope game, Moya and her team did it all. She was one of the most feared and respected bitches in the streets.

Moya was a gangsta through and through, and she was battle-tested. She was one of a kind.

After witnessing her father get murdered ten years ago—two days before her twelfth birthday—it changed her life dramatically. Especially after being shot in the process and haunted by continual nightmares, it forced Moya down a path that many have yet to come back from.

After burying her husband, Naomi relocated back to Jacksonville, Florida, which is where she's originally from. Once again, she had to raise her daughters by herself with the little help provided by Roland's sister and mother. The next couple of years after her husband's death were tough for Naomi. But she still made a way and did the best she could to keep a roof over her family's head and food in their mouths. She worked two jobs and did hair on the side to make ends meet. Until Moya made it her business to step in and become the black sheep of the family.

It all started off with her beef at fourteen years old with the little sister of a gangsta. That very same gangsta was affiliated with the city's notorious street gang called the Kut-throats. His name was Kutt C.J., and he was well-respected all around Duval County. Moya built her rep, starting in school and rising to bustin' heads and wreaking havoc in the streets against Kutt C.J.'s affiliates. Before long, her gangsta was noted and respected, and then she was taken under the wings of Kutt C.J. From there, Moya was introduced to a whole 'nother lifestyle of gangbangin' and puttin' in work to earn her keep.

Years later, after Moya had solidified her reputation at the age of seventeen, Naomi couldn't keep up with her, and neither could her own organization. When Kutt C.J. realized that he had created a monster in Moya, there was nothing he could do to tame her. But she was loyal to her crew, and they loved her immensely. Then a shooting incident where three people were shot at a party, and one of them died, almost ruined Moya's whole existence. The cops were constantly on her ass, harassing her and her family. She had been the streets' talk, and that placed Moya in a critical position. So much so that her mother sent her off to Tallahassee, where Roland's mother, Ella Mae, looked after her until things died down. But that only turned her up more, and within no time, Moya was raising hell in the streets.

That's when she bumped into Tito in a dark alley one evening, battered and bruised, having been the object of terror because of his association with another nigga who had robbed the wrong nigga. That night Moya took him in and helped nurse him back to good enough health to get those same niggas back who had got him. From that moment, the two had been almost inseparable. Moya and Tito had come a long way together in the streets. He was a friend, a brother— Tito was her heart. And for him, she would set the world on fire.

Years later, up until that very day, Moya and Tito had built one of the strongest empires in the city—a team full of young niggas who hustled hard and would kill you in a heartbeat.
And Moya was queen of them all.

"Take me to see Bizkit over at the spot," said Moya, referring to one of her loyal shooters who ran her trap house over in South City.

"Are you sure you wanna deal wit' that right now? We got that meetin' wit' David to attend."

"About my money? Hell yeah! I don't give a fuck if I was meetin' wit' Jesus, I'ma straighten a bitch 'bout my paper, Tito. Obviously, Bizkit can't do his job correctly, so I'm gonna show him how shit needs to be done," said Moya aggressively.

"But we meet wit' David in fifteen."

"He can wait," said Moya. "That muthafucka needs me, not the other way around."

Tito didn't press her further and directed the Mustang toward the south side of Tallahassee. Last time they were in that area together, a church reverend was killed, and now it was all on the news.

"I won't be long, I promise." Moya sipped her drink.

"Say no more," he answered humbly.

***

Toya was busy grading schoolwork in her classroom during recess when two fifth graders entered the room. Both girls, Toya knew, were Keyonna Bradwell and Royalti Andrews. She knew by the looks on both of their faces that the two pretty girls were up to something. Toya removed her smart glasses and set her ink pen aside.

"Why aren't you two at recess?" asked Toya.

It was Royalti who answered. "Because we are on a quest," she replied.

"A quest?"

Both girls nodded.

"And what does this quest have to do with you being in here right now?" Toya sensed some form of trickery going on between the two girls. Then they each grabbed her by the arms, pulled her up to her feet, and told her that there was a surprise for her.

"What surprise?" she wanted to know. "What's going on?"

"Just come with us and you'll see, Ms. Scott," said Keyonna, tall and lanky for her young age. And then Toya was led away and out of her room.

A minute later, Toya was led away from the building outside to the school's playground, where she indeed got the surprise.

Right next to the sliding board and monkey bars in the grassy area of the premises sat her boyfriend, Elijah, upon a beach towel with a basket containing food and chilled beverages to make out the fixings of a picnic.

"Elijah," said Toya in astonishment as the two girls brought her to rest before him. "What are you doing?"

"About to have a picnic with the most beautiful woman in the universe." Elijah was dressed in his usual casual attire of a crisp white button-down shirt, Amiri slacks, and a pair of loafers. He stood up and gave each one of the girls five-dollar bills and thanked them kindly before shooing them off. As the girls skipped away, Elijah took Toya by the hand and helped her down onto the ground, where he began setting out the food and stuff.

"You never cease to amaze me, Elijah." For a year now, that's all Toya had been experiencing from Elijah—one special moment after the other, and there's never been a boring moment between them.

"I'm just tryna make you smile, baby."

"But here at my job, though? And how did you manage to find those two knuckleheads to play a part in all this? Of all the children here at this school, you chose Keyonna and

Royalti?" Toya shook her head and watched as Elijah set out a bowl of grapes and strawberries, tuna fish sandwiches, Doritos chips, and a variety of pastries along with her two favorite drinks.

"I remember you tellin' me how they helped you get settled in when you first started." Toya knew the two girls as being pranksters and had told Elijah about her initial meeting with the girls. Both Keyonna and Royalti were partners in crime, and on Toya's first day as a teacher at Sable Palm Elementary, she had become the object of the girls' relentless pranks.

Toya would never forget that fateful day several months ago; she had been both humiliated and bested by two fifth graders at school.

"But," Elijah added with a grin, "a magician never reveals his secrets."

"Child, please!" Toya waved off his statement. "You wouldn't know how to do magic to save your damn life."

"How much you wanna bet I do?"

"You know magic?" Toya gave him a side-eye.

He nodded.

"Show me, then."

"What's behind your ear?" whispered Elijah, reaching over to lift her shoulder-length hair away from her right ear and touching it.

"Whateva, Elijah!" She rolled her eyes. Then she felt something tickle the inside of her ear and cringed away from him. To her surprise, between his fingers was a beautiful 5-carat diamond gold ring, sparkling brilliantly. Toya gasped at the ring and reached for it, and he pulled back.

"I told you I know magic." Elijah took her by the hand and slipped the ring onto her finger.

A tear trickled from her eye down her cheek as she allowed the moment to overwhelm her. Then that one fateful night ten years ago reminded her just how important this very moment was to her. And Elijah knew exactly what this moment meant to her; he planned to fulfill his promises of love and devotion and make her whole.

Back in the hood, Moya and Tito pulled up outside the trap house on Magnolia Drive. They parked at the curb and got out. Posted up outside on the front porch of the house was one of Moya's youngins, Tyree, who was maintaining his position as the trap house lookout and guard.

Upon their approach, Tyree gave the front door the code knock, and it opened. He held the door open for Moya to enter first, who didn't even acknowledge his presence and stepped over the threshold.

Inside the trap house, Bizkit was in the kitchen cooking crack and bagging up heroin alongside Little PJ. Spud, the second shooter whose job was to guard inside and rotate shifts with Tyree, was the one who opened the door and did not alert the others of Moya's presence. She entered, Spud gave her a nod in the kitchen's direction, and Moya walked straight in there, startling them both inside.

"Oh shit," said Moya with a straight face. "Did you handle that situation this morning like I asked you to, Bizkit?" She directed her attention to the eighteen-year-old hustler with the Boosie fade haircut and Dumbo ears.

"It's handled, Mo," said Bizkit.

"So where is my money?" Moya had been informed the evening before that one of her trap house workers, Don-Don, had been tricking off with her product with hoes and hookers. The young nigga was a cousin of a close associate of hers, and she gave him a shot on face value alone. Lately, Don-Don had been coming up short with Moya's money, and since Bizkit was her trap house lieutenant, it was his responsibility to rectify the problem concerning the trap house.

"I don't got no money, Mo," he said.

Moya sized him up like she wanted some smoke.

"I got blood," Bizkit replied.

That's when Bizkit beckoned her to follow him and led her to the bathroom. Stretched out along the inside of the tub, bloody and dead as a doorknob, was sixteen-year-old Don-Don. Apparently, he had been stabbed to death right there where he lay.

"He kept giving me bullshit excuses, so I gave him what comes wit' it," said Bizkit, standing in the bathroom doorway next to Moya. Tito then peered over her shoulder into the bathroom and shook his head sadly.

"When night falls, dispose of him," was all Moya had to say about the matter before she headed back to the door to take her leave. There was nothing else to talk about; she had been paid, and Don-Don's debt was cleared.

"What about Trap?" said Tito once they were back inside the car out front.

"What about him? They both knew what they signed up for," said Moya. "You play wit' my money and you die, simple." She reached for her red cup and took another sip of her drink and said, "And the same goes for David Marshall too. Now take me to him so I can see if he's ready to die as well."

"Say no more, my nigga."

Chapter 3

Another round of putting her sex game down on Zamon put him right to sleep. Joya was far from tired; she was long-winded and built to last. Fucking was what she did best; it was sport to her, and she enjoyed the power her pussy had over people—men in general.

Which was why she utilized that time to reconnect with another one of her marks who'd been blowing her phone up. She couldn't answer him at the time because Zamon was trying to blow her back out. Joya went into the bathroom and locked the door behind her. She turned on the shower and sat down on the toilet to place her call, warning herself not to speak too loud where Zamon could overhear her phone conversation.

"Yes, Roman. We're still on for this evening, my love. I told you I'll be ready by six o'clock. If you let me go now, I can clear the rest of my appointments and then be ready to love you down later after dinner. Yes, Roman. I understand, Roman. Bye, love." Joya ended the call on her Galaxy cell phone and exhaled softly.

Roman "Rome" Taylor was the newest big-time dope boy in the making in Valdosta, Georgia. He controlled some major parts of its areas and everything that surrounded it.

Roman had the streets on lock with some new exotic drug called "Rated-R." After bumping into Roman a month ago in Atlanta at Magic City while seeking potential marks, she'd been hooking up with him once a week, and every visit he broke her off proper. There was nothing like some good out-of-town pussy, and she had that nigga wide open for the nookie. At their last meeting, she let him fuck her in the ass, and she got ten bandz afterward. Roman was something special, and she planned to keep him satisfied.

The sound of the doorbell reverberated throughout the house, snatching Joya out of her reverie. She rose up from where she was sitting and paused. Should she answer the door or pretend she was actually taking a shower? Joya wondered, figuring Zamon would awaken wake up and do it, or maybe he was already up. Joya decided on the latter and hopped into the shower to freshen up.

Later, Joya entered the living room dressed in a pair of LV loungewear shorts and sandals to show off her pedicured feet. A broad grin appeared on her face when she saw her friend Vonda occupying the room with Zamon. This was her road dawg, her ace, and one of the few bitches besides her siblings who she trusted the most.

"Look who's finally her made her way back home," teased Joya as she opened out her arms to her friend. "I see your trip down in to the Florida Keys done made your black ass extra crispy wit' that tan, bitch!"

Vonda indeed was a black muthafucker, but pretty and with much sex appeal. Today she was rocking a tan Escada skirt with a matching blouse and Jimmy Choo pumps, looking like she was really on her corporate shit.

Zamon yawned and stretched out along the sofa, admiring the view of two beautiful bad bitches in his presence. He couldn't help looking at Vonda's big round ass, like a basketball was underneath her skirt. When he felt his dick hardening, he shifted his attention toward the TV, where a rerun of *Paid in Full* was viewing playing on the Bounce network channel.

Joya caught him checking her girl out but didn't trip. Instead, she hooked an arm through Vonda's, and together they entered her bedroom they entered her bedroom. She was far from the jealous type because she considered herself a winner. She knew the animalistic nature of men—the dog in them—and with that, she would utilize their own nature against them. Niggas ain't shit, and bitches neither, so she respected the game for what it was and never tripped about it.

"So what's the play?" Joya asked her friend once they were in the room, and Vonda told her all about her road trip down south.

"His name is Official Campbell."

"Official?" Joya stared at her questioningly. "What type of nigga would name himself Official?"

"Because that's exactly what he is, Toya. Official. And the nigga got money longer than train smoke." When Vonda said those words, she had Joya's undivided attention. She was already plotting on her next come-up.

***

That afternoon Toya was beaming like the happiest woman in the world could be. Elijah had proposed to her in marriage on the elementary school playground, and she said yes. It took her a minute to get past the shock, but after seeing the diamond rock on her finger, on top of Elijah leaning in to place a kiss on her lips, she accepted his proposal. If they weren't on school grounds, she would have jumped on the dick right then and there. She loved Elijah, and he was the best thing to happen to her in a very long time.

As always, Toya, along with some of the other dedicated teachers, was seeing the children off for the day. Toya was making sure the little ones got their right school bus, directing traffic, and even breaking up after-school scuffles between two of the older kids. She loved her job. Toya was also a favorite, let the little ones tell it. But as she was orchestrating safety procedures with a few wild, reckless ones, something told Toya to look up. When she looked up and surveyed the area, she spotted someone familiar crossing the street over onto the sidewalk. That someone was none other than Desiree Smith, still dragging along with her head down and a pained look on her face.

For a long moment, Toya just stood there watching the lone figure of Desiree walking away. Her heart warmed with concern. Desiree moved her deeply.

Before she could stop herself, Toya was hurrying along the walkway and crossing the street over to the other side. The girl was up ahead by at least twenty yards, and Toya called out after her.

"Dez!" Toya watched as the girl looked over her shoulder at her and recognized who it was. Desiree quickly turned back forward and continued to press onward. Earlier, when she had a little spare time left to do some research, Toya revisited Desiree's life. There she learned that the girl lost her mother a little over a year ago. It was a tragic death resulting from an alleged suicide involving a loaded gun and suspicions that the husband played a role. Even some of the teachers believed Brodrick Smith had been abusing his wife for years, which led up to him losing her in death by a gunshot to the head. That was enough for Toya to suspect Desiree's father of abusing her for whatever reason. But even that was sketchy because the girl never spoke on such things, nor had she been so emotionally guarded before as she was now.

Toya believed the girl was lying to her earlier when she said she was just experiencing a stomach ache. It just did not feel right to Toya.

"Desiree!" Toya called out to her again, and Desiree did not even look back this time. She turned on the next street up ahead and seemed to have sped up to put more distance between them. When Toya noticed this, she took off in a light jog to catch up with the girl. Good thing she was wearing flats instead of heels, and Toya closed the distance between them.

"What do you want wit' me?" Desiree suddenly stopped and whirled around on Toya, looking into her beautiful hazel eyes and seeing a faint sparkle in them.

"I'm worried, Desiree," she told the girl.

"Worried about what?"

"You," said Toya. "Worried about you not being truthful with me. Not only am I your teacher, but I'm your friend too. We are friends, right?"

"I can't have . . . I mean I don't want no friends," said Desiree. Her statement touched Toya, but she already knew the girl was just scared of something.

"You have Jamaal and Alexis," she noted.

"That's all I need, Ms. Scott."

Right then, the front door of a white house with a gate surrounding it opened. There stood a big bear of a man, glaring out after them and yelling for Desiree to get in the house. The boom in his deep voice all but frightened the hairs off Desiree; she was scared to death of him, and Toya knew a bully when she saw one too.

Desiree turned away from Toya and made her way inside the front gate of the house. And Toya was right on her heels behind her.

"No. Go away!" Desiree glanced back and whispered frantically at her, the golden hue reflecting in her bright eyes.

"It's okay," Toya told her.

Moments later, the girl was slipping past her father into the house and Toya confronted him face to face. She stood there on his doorstep and glared into his eyes, letting him know without saying that she wasn't a punk bitch.

"Who the hell are you?" he demanded.

"I'm Desiree's teacher, Toya Scott," Toya answered firmly.

"What the hell do you want?" he sneered. Brodrick looked like the type of man who was used to violence.

32

It was then that Toya told him about Desiree's "alleged" stomach ache and that she thought he should consider checking her in to receive some kind of medical attention.

"She'll be a'ight," said Brodrick. "That girl always complaining 'bout somethin' or the other. What she needs to do is stop being so damn weak and toughen up!"

"She's a child, Mr. Smith."

"Get the hell outta my face, woman! Tellin' me what I should do about my own damn child." When he stepped back to shut the door in Toya's face, she stuck her foot out to prevent him from doing so.

"I want you to hear this and hear it good, Mr. Smith. Do not let me find out you are mistreatin' that poor girl in there. Because I know somethin' you don't know, and it got nothing to do with the law or Family Services. Consider this a warning." Toya gave the door a brute shove and turned around and walked away.

"Bitch!" Toya heard Brodrick say behind her back, and she didn't even give him the satisfaction of getting another response out of her.

If only he knew how profound her warning was.

Later that night, while Bizkit was seeing to the disposal of Don-Don's body, Moya was pulling up outside a forest green-colored townhouse. She was now over on the north side of the city, in D-Black territory, making her last round before she took it in for the night. She could afford to go home early while her youngins were out there making her money bag larger by the minute. She had to stop by and check up on her youngin, Flame, who was finishing up his house arrest status. Her little nigga was going through it— he wanted to be in them streets. Flame was missed in them trenches.

Before stepping out of the car, she removed the lock from the safety of her Glock .21 first. Moya made sure a round was in the head, then she opened the door and got out. You can't be too careful out there in them streets; niggas always getting caught lackin'. Not her, because she was always on point.

"My nigga," Moya said, approaching the doorstep of the house where Flame was sitting and smoking Loud pack. She bumped fists with him and took a seat next to her youngin. "How ya livin', Flame?"

Flame was a seventeen-year-old go-getter, one of the realest young niggas Moya knew. He passed her the blunt and said, "I'll be livin' good tomorrow."

"Tomorrow?" Moya looked at him.

"Yeah. They gon' cut this muthafuckin' leg monitor off. I can't fuckin' wait too," he said.

"Wait a minute, my nigga. I thought you had like a month left on house arrest?"

"I did. But they lettin' me off early. Come to find out the bitch that's holdin' me on this shit is one of my lil' chicken's auntie. She put in a good word on my behalf, made me promise her some thangs, and ol' girl hit me up earlier today wit' the news."

Hearing this made Moya smile, and she threw her arm over his shoulders. "We miss you out there."

"I'm back," he said.

"Like you never left!" Moya passed him back the blunt as a crackhead approached them from the street. Moya clutched her Glock tighter and watched the rail-thin dopehead come to rest before them.

Flame served her two dime rocks, and the dopehead hurried off to go administer her fix.

"That's a damn shame," muttered Moya. "Not even twenty years old and already strung out on that dope."

"It's a cold world out there."

Moya nodded. "And it's about to get colder, I can feel it, Flame," she said.

"That's why I'm gon' turn the heat up!"

"I know," she grinned over at her youngin. "That's why they call you Flame."

Chapter 4

The following morning, Toya woke up earlier than usual, went out and ran her usual three miles, showered, and prepared for another day educating the youths of today. But today she moved with a new purpose, despite the pleasurably throbbing sensation between her legs after going three rounds of sexual healing with Elijah last night. The nigga put it down and almost had her walking bowlegged—it hurt so damn good. She was about to be a married woman to the man she loved, and life couldn't be more beautiful.

That feeling was short-lived when Toya noticed that Desiree hadn't shown up for first period this morning. She waited a little while longer, and by the end of the class, she was forced to page the principal, Amanda Fry.

Principal Fry promised that she would phone Desiree's house to see if she could reach anybody. By third period, with no response from the principal, Toya decided to take matters into her own hands.

During her hour break at recess, Toya requested and located Desiree's house number and her father's cell number. Some might say Toya was just overreacting, but she had no clue that what she was feeling was deeper than rap. When calling the house, she got no answer, then tried Brodrick's phone and got his voicemail, which encouraged her to try his work number.

"Go to hell!" Brodrick hung up on her when she finally reached him at his workplace. And that was all the evidence Toya needed to believe some foul play was behind Desiree's absence.

Toya took off for the girl's home, which was just a short distance away; she lived right around the corner from the school. Once there, Toya banged on the front door. When she got no answer, she made her way around the house, peeking into every window that might reveal any clue as to what was going on inside. If Desiree was actually home and not answering the door, it only meant she had been told not to by her father and was scared to do so. Or maybe she wasn't home, but personally, Toya doubted that the girl would be allowed to skip school without any plausible reason for doing so.

And that's where Toya found her, through the bedroom window, curled up in her bed half-naked. Toya called out to her, and Desiree slowly lifted her head to look in her direction. What Toya saw—or what she thought she saw— was enough to make her heart stop for at least one whole second.

"Oh God! No!" Toya cried out and stormed back toward the front door, giving it another good pounding before ramming her shoulder into it in an attempt to force it open. "Dez, open the door, honey! Please! I'm here to help you, I won't let no one hurt you! Please, I need you to open up for me. Please, Dez!" There were tears in her eyes.

After what seemed like forever, the front door opened, and there stood Desiree in just a pair of filthy underwear.

Toya gasped, and the girl swayed on her feet before Toya caught her.

"My side . . ." Desiree sobbed into Toya's arms. "He pushed me down the steps. I can't breathe right . . . It hurts . . . so bad," cried the girl as she clung desperately to Toya, who was also crying.

"Okay, baby girl. I gotcha. I'm here now." Toya lifted the child up into her arms and carried her inside. Then she called for help, and when the paramedics came, Desiree begged Toya not to leave her.

Toya rode with her all the way to Tallahassee Memorial Hospital. On their way there, Toya was informed that Desiree was apparently experiencing the pain of two cracked ribs. The girl looked so small and broken that it literally broke Toya's heart.

Upon their arrival at the hospital, Toya's cell phone rang with an incoming call from Moya. As the paramedics were carting Desiree away on a gurney, Toya answered her sister's call with a grudge.

"Are you okay, Twin?" Moya asked.

"No! I'm not, Moya," snapped Toya. "I'm pissed!"

"I knew it, I felt that shit." Moya could apparently sense when the other was experiencing some form of pain or another. "What's wrong?"

"I need you to come get me from the hospital."

"The hospital?"

"Yes. And make sure you bring 'that thang' with you too," said Toya with malice in her voice.

A brief pause followed.

"I never leave home wit'out it. I'm on the way!" And when she came, all hell was about to break loose. But the damage was already done, and there was no way Toya could prevent the storm that was coming for Brodrick Smith after what he did.

***

Naomi had just stepped out from her Sherwood residence in Jacksonville when she received a call from the last person she was prepared for, especially after more than a decade of no contact, but she listened to what they had to say.

When she was told to stop whatever she was doing and come back to Tallahassee, that Moya's life depended on it, Naomi did just that. She had spoken with Toya that same morning, and she assured her that all was well with the family. But after receiving the call from the Professor, aka Anthony Lucci, the former Italian drug lord and business mogul who was once Roland's loyal connect and good friend, Naomi realized there was more going on behind the scenes where Moya's well-being was concerned. The Professor was well-connected and respected in the underworld through secret societies where most of the biggest street dealings are handled. So when he said to come, there was no reason for her to doubt that whatever he had to say was worth the two hours she would have to endure to reach Tallahassee.

A black SUV had already been waiting outside her house to drive her there. Naomi didn't even ask any questions; she just got in and prepared herself for the ride.

The Professor warned her not to contact Moya or any of her children until after he had spoken his piece. He needed her to understand the dangers of the situation, and Naomi didn't need to be told twice.

Two hours later, Naomi was taken to a large gated estate home not far from the Governor's mansion. The Lucci Estate was set on top of an imposing hill. It was a sprawling three-story structure of brick, stone, and clapboard surrounded by acres of emerald grass and dotted with mature trees. It emphasized old money, though the mounds of money that had built it were only thirty years old. The black SUV stopped at a pair of massive wrought-iron gates. There was an automatic security sentry guarding the entrance, and he waved the truck forward after the driver was quickly identified.

"Welcome to Casa Lucci," said a large, well-muscled middle-aged Italian who suddenly appeared at the front door of the huge house to greet Naomi.

Naomi nodded in response and was led through the house, looking around at the breathtaking interior. A minute later, she was led to an extraordinarily large home study equipped with what appeared to be thousands of books lining the spacious walls upon big bookshelves.

"It's been a long time, Naomi," said the Professor, who had been sitting behind a great corporate desk. He was a big man in his mid-sixties, dressed in a burgundy cardigan sweater, white shirt, muted tie, and black slacks.

"What is this about, Anthony?" Naomi didn't have time for small talk and wanted to get to the meat of the matter. "What's this mess you told me about my daughter being in danger?"

Without saying a word, the Professor leaned forward and brought up a walkie-talkie device.

"Tito!" Naomi stiffened at the name. The only Tito she knew was the one from the Jackson Five, and Moya's right-hand man. Then her surprise took a whole other turn when the double doors to the home study opened, and in came Tito Shaw, carried by two serious-looking henchmen.

"As you can see, my dear, for me to have taken it to this level, he's obviously been in the wrong."

"What did he do?" asked Naomi.

"I'll tell you what he did," another voice answered from beyond the double doors just before Patrick Lucci appeared in the doorway. At the sight of the man who was the Professor's son, Naomi felt her heart quicken in her chest. "Tito here has been working with the government to help build a case on our daughter and her whole organization."

Naomi swallowed nervously and shot a glance in the Professor's direction. Her secret was now out, and she didn't know how this situation would turn out.

"Don't sweat the fact that I know your daughters are my biological grandchildren," said the Professor. "I could care less about the affair you and Patrick had behind Roland's back. What's more important is the trouble Tito here is trying to create for us all."

41

Naomi shot another nervous glance over at Patrick, who was the one who had personally dealt with Roland in their drug deals. Naomi still couldn't believe she had allowed herself to get involved with Patrick. But he had been there for her when she was most vulnerable, when Roland was on the run, and one thing had led to another.

Roland was not the triplets' real father, and it killed Naomi inside for years, keeping the truth from him. Now she really felt like shit.

Suddenly, the loud, petrifying scream that erupted from Tito snatched her out of her reverie. When she turned back to look, she saw Tito's already battered and bloody face, and she cringed at the sight before her. Naomi watched as one of the henchmen reached in, took hold of his tongue, and ripped it right out of his mouth. The savagery of the act almost made Naomi's stomach turn.

"Take him out back and kill him," the Professor ordered his men, and they did as they were told.

Shaken by the act of violence that had just transpired before her, Naomi turned her gaze back to the Professor and said, "Wouldn't his death still hinder her case?"

"No," said Patrick grimly.

The Professor lit up a rich Cuban cigar. "Luckily, one of my contacts in the government knows about the case and has the power to shut it down. With Tito gone, there's no one else's word credible enough to go with."

"But—" Naomi paused.

"There's so much you don't know about Moya, my dear, and now it's time that you should. Because when it's all said and done, you'll know that Moya is Moya, and not a soul in the world can change the fact that her gangsta is her destiny," said the elder Lucci as he sat behind his big desk, smoking his cigar and telling Naomi everything she needed to know.

And then a gunshot rang out in the distance.

Naomi shivered.

It was then that Tito lost his life.

***

Prior to Naomi receiving the Professor's phone call, Moya found herself lying on the floor in the back of Brodrick's old Dodge Magnum.

When she reached the hospital and saw Desiree all sad and broken up, that inner demon awakened in her. All Toya had to do was give her Brodrick's name, and she promised her that she would handle it from there.

Moya was about to kill this nigga for what he did to Desiree. She didn't play that shit, and Brodrick was about to get punished for his actions. As soon as that nigga got behind the wheel, she was gonna slit his throat and blow his fucking brains out. That should be any minute now; the call from the hospital would alert him. He had no clue the devil would be present the instant he got his bitch ass in the car.

Then came the cops—three TPD police cruisers—turning into the entrance of the Leon County Printing House. The cop cars came to a halt outside the building's entrance doors, and two police officers hurried inside. Moya watched from beyond the dark tinted windows of the Dodge Magnum and saw two more officers standing outside. She then cussed angrily when she saw Brodrick being escorted from the building in cuffs and placed in the back of one of the cars. For a second, Moya contemplated jumping out with her guns blazing on all of them muthafuckers. She wanted her man, and to hell with whoever was standing in her way from doing so.

"Nigga, you just got blessed," she muttered as she watched Brodrick being driven away.

Her phone rang, and she dug into the pocket of her fitted Purple Brand pants. She hoped it was Tito hitting her back after multiple times trying to reach him. But it wasn't Tito calling at all.

"What's up, Twin?"

It was Toya.

"I'm sorry, but I think you should hold off on that for now," said Toya, and the fear Moya heard in her voice made her frown.

"It's too late for that, Twin."

"Let him breathe, Moya."

"He will for now," Moya told her. "Them crackaz just got his ass. But that's only prolonging the death that I got coming for his ass. No exceptions."

Chapter 5

Joya was exiting the building after concluding her morning class on FAMU campus. She headed straight for the parking lot across camps. Within ten minutes she was sliding behind the wheel of her navy blue '19 Acura NSX and pulling into traffic. She was on a mission, and money was the motive. When she came upon a red light, she utilized that time to place a text message to inform her mark that she was on her way.

The traffic light turned green. she drove through the light and made a right turn into the new industrial business area on North Monroe Street. She then made a sharp right turn in the entrance parking lot and headed towards the second from the last industrial building. When she spotted the sign that read "McTlugh & Associates Law Firm", she swung her car into an empty parking space outside the building.

Upon entering through the entrance door of the law firm, Joya saw a pretty blond-haired young woman sitting behind the large desk counter in the reception hall.

"Excuse me, I'm here to see Mr. Elford Reid." Joya said as she leaned her body against the counter. "I'm Charizma Jones, and I'm on a noon appointment with him."

The receptionist lifted her hands over the keyboard before her and stared into the computer screen. Moments later, she advised Joya to wait a minute because Mr. Reid was in the process of concluding a meeting he was already attending. After waiting about nine minutes, Joya was informed that Mr. Reid had ended his meeting and summoned her.

"Let's do it," sighed Joya and got up and made her way as instructed.

Elford Reid was a partner in the firm, the husband of the founder's niece, and father to her two children. He was fifty-two years old, arrogant, half-Black, and born from money. Recently, he'd won one of the biggest capital murder cases of the last twenty years—the death of a junior politician. After two and a half years of representing his client, Reid had fought the hard battle and emerged victorious.

Without knocking, Joya let herself into the office and locked the door behind her. Then she pulled off the summer dress she was wearing, got down on all fours, and crawled across the lush carpet to the well-dressed man sitting behind the desk. The lawyer unzipped his pants and released his short but hardened penis. Without using her hands, Joya leaned over his lap and sucked all five inches of his dick into her wet mouth.

"Ahhhh . . . Yessss . . ." Reid sighed in pleasure as he leaned back in his leather swivel chair and closed his eyes. Joya was slurping on his dick like a popsicle.

When she'd had her fill of his dick in her mouth, Joya straddled his lap with her back against him. Once he was inside her, she rode him nice and slow. She knew he adored her ass and wanted him to watch as it bounced on top of him. It didn't take him long to grip her hips, grunting and moaning like a bitch as his climax built up. When he reached the brink, she jumped off him, gripped his dick, and stroked it fast with her smooth hand.

"Oh God! Here it comes!" He made an ugly face and squeezed his eyes shut.

"Cum for me, baby! Bust that nut!" she whispered in that soft, sultry voice of hers. When he tensed up, she leaned in and took him back into her mouth.

"Shit!" The lawyer thought he'd pass out. Joya sucked all his nectar into her mouth and spat it into the trash can next to the big desk.

While he was subsiding from his blissful pleasure, Joya took the time to slip back on her dress. This was her fourth meeting with the big-time lawyer, and she always left him satisfied. Today would be different, though, because Reid's playtime had now come to an end.

"There's something I need you to see, big daddy," she said after retrieving her purse and cell phone from the mini law bookshelf next to the door.

"What is it?" asked Reid, setting the envelope upon the desk and pushing it toward her.

That's when Joya showed him the recording on her phone of their secret sexual rendezvous in his office—all four episodes. The man looked like he was about to vomit all over himself. Then he began to sweat profusely, and that's when Joya stated her demands.

"If you care for your wife and career as I know you do, have my fifty thousand dollars in cash by this time tomorrow. No exceptions. Good day, Mr. Reid," Joya said sweetly before making her exit.

It was a dirty game.

If there was anybody Toya trusted at that moment to watch over Desiree without complaint, it was Ella Mae. This was Roland's mother, Toya's grandma and best friend, and without a shadow of a doubt, she knew baby girl would be in good hands. Ella Mae hurried over to the hospital, where she immediately began to rule over the whole situation.

"Thank you for coming, Mama." Toya was emotionally drained and happy to have found the perfect person to look after Desiree. "Your help is greatly appreciated."

"I'm here. Don't fret, child. The Lord is in charge," replied Ella Mae as she stood at Desiree's bedside, watching her sleep soundlessly. "Why would anyone want to hurt this beautiful child?" she murmured.

Toya had told her what happened, and all the old woman could do was shake her head.

By now, Toya knew the school administrator was probably beside himself with worry and had been blowing her phone up. She had to return to the school to give her report and finish the rest of her day teaching. Although she wasn't gonna be as focused as she should be because of her concern over Desiree, Toya had to do what she had to do.

When it was time for her to go, Toya hugged Ella Mae and placed a gentle kiss upon the girl's cheek. Then she made her way over to the door and opened it.

"Where the fuck is she?"

Toya paused in the doorway at the big-bodied, wild-looking woman who suddenly appeared before her. She sized the woman up and braced herself for the confrontation that was coming.

"Excuse me," Toya responded. "Who are you?"

"Is Desiree in there?"

"Once again, lady, who are you?"

"My name is Wanda Smith. I'm Desiree's auntie. I need to get in there and see her, and make sure her little evil ass hasn't told them folks anything crazy," Wanda replied, with aggression laced in her voice. She almost looked like she wanted to square up with Toya or something.

"I can't let you do that."

"Why the hell not?"

"First of all," Toya stepped forward and shut the door behind her, "not with that kinda attitude am I gonna allow you to walk through that door and disturb her."

"Look, bitch. If you don't move outta my way—"

"Or what?" Moya said from behind her, suddenly appearing out of nowhere around the corner. When Wanda turned to see who it was breathing down her neck, she froze in instant astonishment. Then she looked back at Toya and then back at Moya, who was sneering like a vicious hyena. Moya and her twin sister were 100% identical, except for

Moya's bottom row of diamond-encrusted platinum teeth and Toya's black rose tattoo along the side of her neck.

"Y'all can't stop me from going in there." Wanda put on a brave act, but she was nervous as hell.

Without warning, Moya drew her Glock and pressed it against Wanda's front with that wicked look in her eyes. When Toya saw this, she became nervous too, knowing how dead serious her twin was right now.

"I don't give a fuck about you, bitch," Moya hissed as she stepped closer to Wanda. "Your best bet is to kick rocks before I stretch your ass out right where you stand."

"You wouldn't dare," said Wanda.

A deadly smirk crossed Moya's face, and she raised the pistol, putting it to Wanda's head. Instinct kicked in, and Toya lowered her twin's arm and warned Wanda to leave, or else things were gonna pop off. Wanda saw the threat was real and hurried away up the hallway.

"Put that damn gun up, stupid! I gotta get back to the school. Will you take me?"

Moya nodded. "Who was that bitch, Twin?"

"Let's hurry up, because you done stopped all types of traffic in here." Toya took her twin by the arm, hurried her inside the room for a second to speak with Ella Mae, and then they got the hell out of dodge.

In actuality, Toya knew that they wouldn't be able to keep Wanda at bay for long. She was next of kin and had all the right to take Desiree if she really wanted to.

That's what worried Toya and Moya—to have Desiree taken into the custody of the wrong hands, where she would get hurt again.

The twins left the hospital together and were in traffic headed back to Sable Palm Elementary.

Shit just got real.

After dropping her sister back off at the school, Moya headed out to the Tallahassee mall where she was being expected. On her way there, she called Tito's phone for the millionth time, only to get no answer. This worried her because it wasn't like Tito to not answer his phone. It was situations like this that left her suspicious, though she knew whatever the matter was, Tito could handle it.

But she needed him with her on this mission to go check up on her product. After the meeting with David yesterday, he had assured them that the shipment was in place. And that's exactly where Moya was headed now—to see if the shipment had actually landed successfully. And while she was at it, Moya thought it would be good to buy Desiree something very special to cheer her up a little bit. Her heart went out to the little girl, and she would do whatever it took to see that Desiree was safe and sound.

At the mall, Moya was surprised when she found her youngin, Tron, standing outside the same Gucci store she was about to enter. He was posted up, spittin' game with a pretty redbone shorty with crazy dimples, when she rode up on him and bumped fists with him. That's when Tron introduced his lady friend as Princess, and Moya complimented her on her choice of fuckin' with a solid young nigga.

"I gotta take care of some business in here right quick," said Moya when she leaned in his ear. "I need you to keep an eye out for me too."

"You know I gotcha, Mo."

"Be good."

"Fa 'sho!" Tron saluted her.

Moya entered the Gucci store and browsed around for a minute just to make it look good. Then she got the attention of the sales manager, and he discreetly beckoned her to the back behind the counter, into the storage room. It was there that the sales manager, Carlos, showed her the seven bricks of cocaine divided and compressed into false compartments and bottoms of Gucci bags and shoes, and even a suitcase. This was the new shipment method, instead of the common deliveries that could be easily detected as promised. She would send her youngins in on a shopping spree to retrieve the product.

"Everything good, Mo?" Tron asked when she exited from the Gucci store minutes later.

She assured him that all was well and put the call in to BizKit to put a team together and come pull up at the Gucci store for a little shopping. Meanwhile, Tron had ditched his shorty and was escorting Moya around the mall. She loved her youngins, would kill for her babies, and they all would definitely do the same for her.

"You heard from Tito today?" asked Moya.

Tron shook his head no.

She sent Tito's phone another text message and hoped like hell her man was good. And then she bumped into Jon Boi and two of his boys in the mall. This was a nigga she knew since she was little, one of the many niggas who also wanted her. But Moya respected his gangsta, thought he was a standup nigga, but would not let his charming personality knock her off her square like he do so many others.

There was only one nigga who could get that pussy, and Jon Boi wasn't him.

Her shit was cherishable.

It was pressure.

And then the call came. Moya rushed out of the mall.

And straight to the hospital she went once again.

Chapter 6

The look on her face was priceless. Naomi couldn't believe the things the professor had shared with her. But she was glad that he had brought those things to her attention, because she would have been in the blind if anything had happened to Moya. And she already knew Moya was a street bitch, a killer, and Naomi blamed herself for not being a better mother. But she knew from the moment Moya experienced her father being killed and suffering in the process that she was gonna grow up and cause hell on earth.

Naomi knew Moya better than anybody, which is why she allowed her dark path to be traveled on her own. Moya was destined to survive the greatest of battles, and she would continue to do so.

When Naomi left the professor's estate, she was anxious to see her children. It had been nearly a year since she saw them, and now was no better time to do so. Riding in the backseat of the sedan driven by one of the professor's men, Naomi stared out her side window in deep thought. But those thoughts were suddenly interrupted when the car came to a stop at an intersection five blocks from the Lucci Estate. The rear doors of the SUV in front of them opened, and three armed men jumped out. Naomi was just about to call Toya when the first blast erupted. The round shot through the windshield of the car by the gunman blew half of the driver's face off. Then Naomi was snatched from the backseat of the car and roughly dragged away.

A minute later, Naomi found herself sitting between armed goons in the backseat of a black Mercedes-Benz. There was another one behind the wheel and in the front passenger seat. It was cold in the car—or was it just her nerves?

"Who are you? What do you want from me?" Naomi asked.

No one bothered to answer her questions.

Guess they were antisocial too, Naomi thought as she studied the men surrounding her. One was Black, another Spanish-looking, and the other two appeared to be Italians. She'd been dealing with them so long Naomi knew what they looked like.

After watching the road, Naomi noticed that they were taking her out of the city limits. Before long, she saw that they were headed towards Quincy, which was located in the next county over. Naomi knew Gadsden County well; she had a few old friends who still lived out there. Her brother Tony used to live out this way. But it wasn't Quincy she was being taken to exactly; it was Midway, which sat just between Quincy and Tallahassee. Naomi was taken through a few roads off the main interstate and into a secluded area where not much traffic transpired. But it was a townhouse residence off in the woods, surrounded by trees and quietness. That's where their journey finally came to rest. Was this where she was about to die? If so, why have his own man murdered in the process?

"Get out," said one of the goons who was sitting next to Naomi, as he got out.

Naomi got out of the car and was led through the back door to the house, two in front of her and the remaining two coming up behind her. The house was silent, and as they led her up front, she saw something that made her mouth drop in absolute surprise.

"Anthony?" she whispered.

"No, my dear," said the man sitting in the wheelchair, who appeared to be paralyzed from the neck down. "I am nothing like my brother, Anthony. Have a seat," he told Naomi.

Automatically, she sat down with a dumbstruck expression on her face. "What's going on?" asked Naomi. She had just left him back at the mansion twenty minutes ago.

Twins, she said to herself. The Professor had a twin. But this one had Naomi transfixed; he scared her a little, though.

"We have a lot to discuss, Naomi," he said. "Particularly my brother."

***

Moya had just stepped out of Desiree's room to take a call when she saw Jon Boi pass by up ahead. She had forgotten all about her phone call and moved up the hallway to go see where he was headed.

Just a little while ago she'd seen him in the mall, and now here he was again. But what was he up to now? she wondered as she turned the corner into the path he was journeying down. Jon Boi looked like he was on a mission.

What the fuck am I doing? Moya halted.

That same instant, her cellphone buzzed in her hand as a text message came through. It was a number she didn't recognize, but the message said for her to call immediately, that it was urgent.

Moya called the number to see what was up.

"Somebody from this number just texted Moya?" she asked as she pressed along up the hallway.

"Yes. This is Bang from over in D-Block," he said.

"What's up, Bang?"

"You still fuckin' wit' that boy Tito, right?"

"That's my man, why?"

"Well, your man just dropped off on my territory, and it ain't looking good for him," said Bang, whom Moya now remembered ran a certain section on the northside, pushing a little weight, but not no kingpin status shit like Devon and 'em from Joe Lewis apartments.

"What do you mean it ain't lookin' good, Bang?"

"I mean dead, homegirl."

"Dead?" Moya stopped walking. When those four letters exited his mouth, Moya instantly began breathing fire. Tito couldn't possibly be dead; she had just spoken with him this morning. She had sent him to go retrieve that money from that nigga Wanky who had been coming up short on his weekly payment. Wanky was from her old neighborhood, and Moya was extorting the nigga for a certain percentage of the money he had coming in from serving dope on her block.

Nigga thought she was bullshitting about selling dope on the same corner her childhood home was on. The house was paid for and still rightfully her mother's; someone else was just living in it now, raising their family.

"How dead do you need me to put it, Moya?" Bang said.

Then he explained to her how Tito appeared to be beaten within an inch of his life and shot dead, then dumped out of an unknown van before it sped off.

"Don't let me find out you niggas over there did this."

"We had nothing to do with that, Moya. So don't bring that bullshit over here on my turf," he said.

She frowned. "Say what, nigga?" Moya felt offended.

"Look, Moya, I don't want no problems with you," he said. "Just don't make my shit hotter than it already is right now."

"I'll see you in a minute, Bang!" she warned him.

"Moya—"

"Ain't no more talkin'!" she said and hung up the phone on him. Then there was a tap on Moya's shoulder, and when she turned around, she came face to face with a male staff.

"What, cracka!" she barked at him. "What the fuck you want?"

"Cellphones are not permitted on this floor, ma'am," said the big man. "Hospital's policy!"

Moya looked at him sideways and punched his big ass in the nose, gushing blood everywhere. "Don't put your muthafuckin' hands on me," she said. "That's my fucking policy!"

Suddenly, Jon Boi came out of nowhere when the man started yelling for security. He didn't care about her policy and took her by the arm, pulling her away from the scene. He damn near had to throw her into the elevator.

"Get your goddamn hands off me, nigga!" she snatched away from him and shoved him hard in the chest.

Jon Boi stepped into her space, all up close and personal, glaring down at her like he wanted some pressure. "I ain't the rest of them niggas out there you got scared of you, Moya. But one thang you're gonna do is respect my muthafuckin' mind! You ain't the only muthafucker going through something, so you better check that shit when you fuckin' with me."

"Who the fuck you talkin' to like that, nigga?"

"You!" he shot back.

They glared at one another, both of them breathing hard and with fire in their eyes. They looked like they wanted to fight.

"Test me," Jon Boi challenged her.

Moya was sneering like a vicious cobra as she stared up at him. Her hand eased towards her waist, but she remembered that her pistol had been taken from her earlier.

"You wouldn't do it even if you was strapped," he said.

"What makes you think that?"

He smirked. "This why," he said, then he leaned down and pressed his lips against hers, kissing Moya with deep passion. His unexpected gesture shocked her for a moment, then Moya gave in to his demand for another moment. Then, another moment later, she had Jon Boi wheezing in agonizing pain after kneeing him hard in the nuts.

"That's the last time you'll taste these lips, muthafucka!" Moya said before the elevator doors opened and she walked out.

Jon Boi was still wheezing in the corner of the elevator, holding his precious jewels, glaring after Moya as she headed for the exit doors out the hospital.

***

When he peered into the car, Detective Shane Rogers found a body slumped across the front seat with half of its head blown off. There was no way to identify the man other than him being possibly white or something close to it.

Next to him, taking pictures of the body, was Inspector Benny Stewart, one of the best crime scene investigators in the city. It wasn't until he moved over to the other side of the car to get shots from another angle that he suddenly froze.

"Um, Lieutenant?"

"Yeah?" Rogers looked up at Benny.

"I think we got something back here you might need to have a look at," said the inspector. He was standing in the open doorway of the back passenger side door, staring into the car with an anxious look on his face.

"What you got?" Rogers said, hearing the ringtone.

Benny pointed at the cell phone lying on the back seat, and it was in the process of ringing with an incoming call. But it was the picture that showed up on the phone's screen that gave the detective pause.

It was a face he would never forget.

Though he thought the face on the screen belonged to Moya herself, it was actually Toya's, and she was in the process of calling her mother's phone.

"Are you gonna answer it?" asked Benny.

Without hesitation, Detective Rogers reached to grab the phone, and as soon as it was in his grasp, it went silent.

Behind him, the crowd of spectators ranted and raved about what was going on and not being able to get through traffic due to the whole area being cordoned off. The incident had taken place at a stoplight along Tharpe Street. Now there were police officers and all types of government officials on the scene.

"I'm calling the number back," said Rogers.

"Is that permitted, Lt.?"

"In my book it is," he replied.

Rogers called the number back for real, and Toya answered the phone on the second ring.

"Hey, Mama. My bad if I woke you up or something. I was just calling to hear your voice and let you know I just sent you some money to your CashApp."

"Is this you, Moya?"

"Who is this?" Toya demanded. "Where is my mama?"

The detective met Benny's intense gaze, then turned back to his phone conversation. Having dealt with Moya on several occasions, he knew without a shadow of a doubt this wasn't her on the other end of the phone. This wasn't Tony Jones' niece.

"Hello? You there?" Toya spoke up again.

"I'm here."

"Whoever this is, please put my mama on the phone."

"I'm sorry," Rogers told her. "I don't think that would be possible at this very moment."

"Who is this?" You could hear the anger in her voice now.

"This is homicide Detective Shane Rogers, Lieutenant Rogers to be exact. Who is your mother, may I ask?"

"Homicide?" Toya sputtered. "Did you just say homicide?"

"Yes. I work for the Tallahassee Police Department. This phone was found on the scene of a crime."

The line went silent.

Rogers looked at the phone and saw that the call was still ongoing. "Are you still there?"

"Please tell me you're bullshittin' with me," she said.

"I wish I was."

"So my mama is here in Tallahassee?"

"To be honest, I don't know where your mother is," Rogers said without emotion, already seeing where this situation was about to go. "But perhaps you could help me find her."

"And how can I do that?" she asked.

"By coming down to the station—" Rogers stopped when he heard the phone disconnect. Then he let out a loud groan in exasperation and shook his head wearily.

Moya was not about to like this shit.

"This is about to get crazy!"

"Why you say that?" Benny replied.

"Because," said the detective, "the mother of one of the most ruthless women in the streets of Tallahassee is involved in an active homicide investigation."

"And missing," added Benny.

Rogers nodded solemnly. "And missing," he whispered.

And all hell was about to break loose.

Hell like never before.

Chapter 7

For a long moment, both Naomi and the Italian just stared at each other without saying a word. Then all of a sudden, the Italian ordered all his men to clear the house and wait outside. There was no hesitation; they all got out.

The house now only occupied him and Naomi.

They had peace and quiet.

"My name is Nicholas Vontelli, born and raised in Brooklyn, New York. The person you call Anthony is William Vontelli, whom you now know as my identical twin brother."

"I've never heard of you," said Naomi.

"You wasn't supposed to, my dear." Nicholas shook his head to prevent her from speaking, and then he continued. "More than thirty years ago, while William and I were sophomores in college, I shared with him my dream of becoming the most powerful biologist the world has ever acquired. And then our father passed, and we both had to travel to Italy, where he was properly buried. We were both the only children and the rightful heirs of all our father's assets he left back in New York.

"After the funeral, William and I returned to the States to situate things according to Father's wishes. But it came to light that he wasn't just your average pizza restaurant owner but something much bigger," he said.

"Your father was into the drug trade," Naomi replied.

Nicholas nodded.

"What happened to you?" she pressed.

Again, the Italian shook his head for her to hush.

"We discovered millions and millions of dollars' worth of heroin in a secret cellar beneath our restaurant. Not really knowing what we were doing, William and I began selling some of the stuff—we were basically giving it away for next to nothing. Until one of our father's buddies came along and taught us the fundamentals of selling heroin. Before long, we were making lots of money, with me being the brains of the operation and William the muscle," said Nicholas before continuing on. "I soon discovered a way to use my biology knowledge to improve the quality of the drug after it had been stepped on a hundred times. For one brick of heroin, which was going for something close to eighty grand wholesale, I would break it down and profit more than a million once I'd worked my magic on it."

"What happened, Nicholas?" Naomi insisted.

He shook his head and let out a deep breath. "William stole the blueprint I had documented and orchestrated a car accident to kill me, but only paralyzed me from the neck down instead," said the Italian in a light whisper.

"Damn," Naomi murmured. "That's fucked up!"

"He took the product, he took my girl, and my dream, and ran away somewhere."

"Here," she said.

"California, New Orleans, and then here," said Nicholas with a deep scowl on his aging face. "And now I've finally caught up with my brother after all these years. But before I see him face to face, I want to destroy his whole operation. I want him to be scared."

Something clicked on in Naomi's mind, and she stared across the room at Nicholas in silent dismay.

"Will you please give me some water, Naomi?" he asked, his tone calm as ever, but his eyes were heavy with emotion after telling his story.

Naomi noticed there was a pitcher of water sitting on a nearby table with a glass and a straw next to it. She fixed him some water with a straw to drink from.

"You're a dear, Naomi," he said gratefully.

"I have a question," she said.

He sucked in more water. "I'm sure you do."

"How much do you know of your brother's operation?"

"Everything."

"Including his business associates and workers?"

"Precisely."

"How long have you known of his dealings here?"

"Why?" he looked at her curiously.

Naomi said, "Because my husband was killed behind this."

"Ah." He nodded. "You're talkin' about Roland."

"You know him?" she perked up.

"My dear, it was Roland who discovered me first, and then I gave him an ultimatum," said Nicholas. "To get out the game or die along with my brother when I came for him."

"What do you mean he discovered you first?"

He knew that she would ask that question next.

"I met Roland up in Jersey sometime after he was released from prison. He thought I was William, and from there the truth came out. The whereabouts of my dear brother and the truth about what he did to me."

"So you told him the same thing you just told me?"

Nicholas nodded. "Roland was a great man, Naomi."

"Then who killed him?"

"Who else had reason to see the great man dead? I mean, c'mon, Naomi. When Roland told William it was over, William had him killed to keep his mind at peace because he knew too much."

Naomi nodded. "That muthafucker!" she growled.

"Right," Nicholas growled too. "And I think he knows I'm here, too. After Roland's murder ten years ago, William retired and went underground. And guess what?"

She looked at him with glazed eyes filled with emotion.

"What?"

"You're the one that helped me find my long-lost twin brother," he said with a smile. "And I can't wait to finally see him."

It was about to go down.

***

Joya sat behind the wheel of her car and stared blankly out the windshield. She didn't know what to do as she replayed the conversation she'd just had with the detective. It was so surreal it wasn't even funny.

Joya called Toya's phone and got no answer.

She wanted to try her mother's number again but was afraid the detective would pick up.

Suddenly, the phone in her hand rang, shattering her current thoughts. Instinctively, she answered the phone without checking who was calling.

"Hello?"

"I'm here," the voice replied.

This was the person Joya had been scheduled to meet up with to conduct business, but the latest occurrence with the mysterious phone call had distracted her. She had forgotten all about the business she had to handle.

"Hi, Lance. I'm sorry. I just pulled up," she said. "I'll be inside in a second." Joya was now undecided about going forward with this meeting, but she'd been looking forward to it for a week now.

A lot of money was riding on this meeting.

Time was of the essence.

Joya wasn't too sure about that mysterious call because she was certain her mother would have notified them first before coming. She didn't know what to believe. So she thought it was best to execute this deal and get on with the other business that had unexpectedly thrown her off guard.

Joya entered the diner, and Lance Winters, the lawyer she was there to meet, raised a hand to get her attention. She moved in his direction through the noisy diner and took her seat across from him.

Lance was one of the youngest partners working out of one of the biggest law firms in the city. But Lance had a thing for young Black women, even though his wife of fifteen years was every man's dream. And Joya was about to teach him a lesson about cheating and having so much to lose in the process.

Money was the motive.

"I'm sorry I'm late," Joya said, reaching across the table to shake his hand in greeting. The look in his eyes said he wanted to fuck, not have no lunch date.

"No need for an apology," he said. "I'm sure you know how to make it up to me."

"Do I?" Joya licked her lips seductively. Then she reached into her purse and slid a manila envelope with his name on it across the table to him.

"What's this?" Lance asked.

"Two hundred and fifty thousand dollars."

Suddenly, the sharply dressed maitre d' came over and took their drink orders. The lawyer waved him off and cast a curious glance across the table at Joya, whose expression was no longer pleasant but firm.

Lance opened the envelope and extracted several photos, but these weren't ordinary photos—they were photos of him and Joya having sex.

"Now, listen, Lance," she began. "This is only business. You're a man of wealth, so if you don't want your wife to get ahold of those pictures, I suggest you cooperate."

"How dare you try and blackmail me with this!" he said, holding up the photos to emphasize his point. But he was already beginning to sweat bullets, which only meant one thing: he was scared and nervous.

"I just did." She rose to her feet. "Have the money by midnight, or your beautiful wife will have reason to milk your ass for everything you got."

"No!" he pleaded. "Don't do this to me!"

"I just did," said Joya before waving at him and strutting towards the exit and out the front door.

By the time she got back inside her car, she found her cellphone ringing. It was Toya calling. "What's going on, sis?" she answered.

"Mama is here!" Toya said.

"Where?"

"Here in Tallahassee, twin."

Joya shook her head. "But where, Toya? Because I got a call earlier from some dude claiming he's a detective, saying that Mama's involved in some homicide case," she said.

"She was," said Toya.

That made Joya pause. "How do you know?"

"Because I'm down at the police station," Toya said. "And I'm looking at Mama's phone right now."

***

Her name was Cindy Gainous, and she was a lovely middle-aged woman with the kindest smile. But at that very moment, Cindy was not smiling. She looked very much scared as she stared down the barrel of Moya's pistol.

That nigga Bang thought she was playing when she said she would see him soon? Didn't he know she was the last muthafucker to be bluffing?

After contacting her government resource and confirming that Tito was dead, Moya went into action. She sought out Bang's mother and was about to do her old ass dirty if she didn't do as she asked. Moya wanted blood for what was done to her main man. Even if Bang didn't have nothing to do with it, she wanted to make him bleed anyway for getting slick out the mouth with her.

Then she was gonna go set the streets on fire.

Retaliation is a must.

"Call your son and tell him to get here now," said Moya, her pistol aimed at the woman's nose.

Cindy regarded her coldly. "I'll never betray my son!"

"Okay." Moya flipped the pistol and bashed her in the eye.

To Moya's surprise, the woman tried to fight back, but she was too much for her. A minute later, Moya was breathing hard as she stared down at the bloody old lady. Cindy was sprawled out on the living room floor, bleeding from multiple wounds. Her bravery cost her pain.

"You can't make me go against my baby," cried the old lady, her mouth spewing blood from her caved-in teeth.

Moya admired her loyalty, but she had no remorse. Then she sent two slugs into her, ending her whole life forever.

Minutes later, after killing Bang's mother, Moya was back on the streets, cruising through his hood like nothing happened. Having run the streets of Tallahassee so much over the years, there wasn't much that she didn't know, especially how to navigate through the most complicated areas on other niggas' turf.

And now it was time to put all that shit into effect now that it was war in the streets. Moya was gunning at every muthafucker Tito had problems with.

Mainly that nigga Wanky, whom she sent him to collect paper from this morning. Then she was gonna take it to those niggas P-Low and Ron's people, just in case they had heat on their chest about Tito shooting those two niggas at the block party recently.

Moya was hurt behind that shit. Tito was her nigga.

"Niggas got the game fucked up," she muttered to herself. Then she noticed somebody tailing her car a little way back. It was a burgundy Infiniti Q30 that took her a minute to recognize. With a shake of her head, Moya reached for her phone and searched through her contacts. Having had his number laid back in her shit for a minute, this would be the very first time she called it.

He answered on the first ring.

"Why the hell are you following me, Jon Boi? Don't you know that shit could get you killed?" she said.

"I'm making sure you—"

"Don't make sure shit, nigga!" she cut in. "Right now ain't the time to be fuckin' with me!"

"I heard what happened to Tito," he said. "My condolences."

She bristled. "I don't need your sympathy, nigga!"

"I'm here whenever you need me, boo. My gun blaze, too!" he said, then disconnected. Moments later, Moya looked over and saw his car flying past her, shooting up the highway.

"When will he ever learn?" she muttered.

Chapter 8

From the backseat of the SUV, Naomi watched as Nicholas' men hefted up his body and situated him into the front passenger seat. The Italian was then secured with the seatbelt and met Naomi's curious gaze in the rearview mirror.

"Remember my promise, my dear," he said.

"One last question, and then I will shut up."

"Ask away," he told her.

The goon, whom she now knew as Carlos, got in behind the wheel of the SUV. This was the Spanish-looking one with the thick mustache who had shot the driver earlier. After being in their presence for so long and earning acceptance from their boss, all of Nicholas' goons were easier on her now than before.

"It's okay to speak," said Nicholas, seeing that she had hesitated when Carlos got in.

She clasped her hands in her lap thoughtfully. "Did you hire my daughter to murder Reverend Harold Banks?"

"I sure did," he answered briskly.

"Why her out of all people? I mean, your own men could have done it," Naomi said.

"Don't ask a question that you already know, Naomi," Nicholas said, but he still went on to explain his reasons why, anyhow. In so many words, he chose Moya for the job because it was a way for her to get back at the person who was responsible for her father's death.

Then she went on to tell him that there was a possibility that Roland wasn't the twins' biological father, but Patrick's, whom she stressed a strong dislike for.

"Roland will always be their father, dear."

Naomi nodded agreeably. "He will always be," she whispered.

For the next fifteen minutes, they conducted small talk until they finally reached Leon County's city limits. They were back in Tallahassee, and their time together was coming to an end. Despite her current predicament, Naomi had to say that she enjoyed the Italian's company.

"Where to next is all up to you, my dear," Nicholas said, referring to where she would like to be dropped off.

She gave them the address to where Toya and Joya lived, though Naomi was a little hesitant to get out of the truck.

"I gave you my word everything will be okay, right?" Nicholas met her intense gaze again.

"You did."

"Then I will honor my word," he said. "Now go be with your lovely family."

"Thank you." Naomi leaned forward to kiss him on the cheek, then she got out of the SUV and hurried towards the apartment building. The truck didn't move until it was confirmed that she was safely inside.

From that point on, it was hunting season for them, while Naomi focused on being there for her daughters.

Naomi found the apartment quiet as a mouse. She then went in search of the house phone but didn't find one. The girls only had cellphones. But there was definitely a laptop computer on the kitchen counter, and Naomi wasted no time sending out an email to all of her children.

A knock at the front door startled her.

Knowing damn well how grave her situation was, Naomi retrieved one of the kitchen knives from the cutting block. She approached the front door with caution. Whoever it was on the other side continued to knock like they knew someone was home.

Was it Carlos or any of Nicholas' other men? Naomi was sure she saw them all drive away after she assured them she was safely inside.

Naomi peered through the peephole and saw a lone female standing there. For a moment, she just watched her to see what she would do. And that's when it hit her—Naomi remembered exactly who this young lady was.

"Shavonda?" said Naomi after opening the door and sticking her head out.

The female had walked away but halted instantly when she heard Naomi call out to her. When she looked over her shoulder, Naomi knew she had hit dead on the money.

"Mz. Naomi," said Vonda.

The twins' mother sighed with relief. This was Joya's homegirl, one Naomi had only met a few times before. At least she had someone to accompany her now.

***

Desiree was in her bed sound asleep when Heather entered the room. Ella Mae looked up from her word search book and greeted her daughter with a kind smile. Without waking the girl, Heather slid a chair up closer to her mother.

"I came as soon as I could," said Heather.

The other woman patted her on the knee. "As long as you're here is all that matters, honey." Then she told Heather about the incident that transpired earlier. "I don't think they could stop that woman from takin' that child if she persists. She is legally the next of kin…"

"What is this woman's name, Mama?" Heather asked.

"Wanda something," she said. "I didn't catch the last name."

Very much aware that it was against hospital policy to have phones, Heather still pulled hers out and began tapping away on its screen.

Desiree's happiness was top priority.

Ella Mae's words were true, and Heather knew it. Not too long ago, a couple of medical staff members came in and checked on the little girl. In a brief conversation with them, the old lady learned a powerful truth that made her own heart troubled.

And that's evidence that Wanda could file for custody of her niece with her brother's consent.

The girl threatened to run away if that happened. After hearing this, it put Heather in a worse mood.

"Damn!" she muttered.

"What is it?"

Heather let out a frustrated breath and continued to peck away at her phone. Whatever she was receiving appeared to not be what she really wanted.

"Tell me something, girl!" Ella Mae said anxiously. "All that pokin' around and not saying nothin' is workin' my dang nerves."

"In a minute, Mama!"

The door opened, and Naomi barged into the room with Vonda hot on her heels. Instantly, the old lady reached for her heart and rose to her feet. Without hesitation, Naomi rushed into her waiting arms. The old lady was so happy to see her, she cried.

"Oh my sweet Lord!" Ella Mae sighed.

Heather stopped what she was doing and fell into Naomi's arms next. There was no mistaking the genuine love they had for each other.

Then the old lady smacked Naomi with her hand, demanding why she waited all this time to come back.

"You know why, Mama," said Naomi.

Ella Mae nodded. "Yeah, I know. But it's good to see you, though, and you still skinny as a string bean!"

They all laughed.

From her bed, Desiree had been awakened by the commotion and was now regarding Naomi with silent curiosity. Toya had told her that her mother was of Dominican descent, and looking at her now, Desiree could see where the twins got their natural beauty from. They all had the same lean figure, caramel skin tone, and long, lustrous black hair that Desiree admired so much. Just lying there watching her teacher's mother interact with the others reminded her so much of the triplets put together. Then Naomi's gaze slid around and locked on the girl's, and a silent communication transpired between them.

Naomi offered her a gentle smile.

She smiled back.

"Have you spoken to the girls already?" asked Heather, bringing the excitement to a calm.

"Yeah," said Naomi. "They're on their way here now." Then she turned to the girl and leaned over the bed rail to stare deeply into her green eyes. "You don't have to worry about a thing anymore, Desiree."

"Why?" Desiree murmured.

Naomi smiled again. "Because your mother was a very good friend of mine. So that makes me more inclined to call you my own, Desiree."

"You knew my mama?"

"Yes. I did know her," Naomi admitted. She still couldn't believe Carla was dead; she had literally cried in the car on her way there after Vonda told her everything. So this wasn't no bullshit just to make the girl feel good—she and her mother had been close for real.

It's a small world.

"You come to take me home with you?" Desiree asked, her pretty green eyes twinkling.

But before Naomi could respond, the door burst open and both Toya and Joya tumbled into the room at once. Naomi wrapped her arms around both of her girls, kissing both of their cheeks tenderly.

"Where's Moya?" Heather wanted to know.

Everybody just looked at one another cluelessly. Only God knew where that damned girl was.

They were four deep in the Chevy Tahoe, watching from a distance as the paramedics carted Bang's mother out of the house in a body bag. From the front passenger seat, Bang clutched his Glock-40 tightly as he watched the only woman he ever loved get wheeled away.

Tears were pouring down his face as his shattered heart began to grow cold in a murderous rage. Bang had been in the streets a long time and had caused his share of pain and agony. But there was nothing like the pain he was experiencing at that very moment. The pain he felt made him wish he was dead too.

But not before causing some bloodshed of his own for what was done to his mother.

He was about to go all out.

And the only person he knew was brave enough to do this was Moya. The bitch had pretty much warned him of this earlier when they spoke. She was one wicked young bitch, one that Bang knew had major weight behind her.

"Ready?" said TK, the one behind the wheel.

Bang was still stuck on Moya and how he was going to handle this situation.

One of them niggas' phones rang in the truck.

"Yo!" It was Boodah in the back who had answered, the one toting the MAC-90 submachine gun. A moment later, he reached the phone out towards Bang. "It's for you, bruh. It's that nigga Real One!"

"Fuck that nigga!" Bang snapped. "Let's ride, TK!"

Boodah delivered the message, listened for a moment, then looked up at Bang and said, "He said it's important, Bang. He say he think he know who offed Mama C.!"

At those words, Bang turned towards Boodah. "What?"

They were rolling behind the coroner's van on their way out of the hood. Bang snatched the phone away from Boodah and put it to his ear.

"Don't play wit' me, Real One!"

"When do you ever know me to play, Bang?" he said.

"Talk!"

"As I was trappin' out Quanda's spot up the way, I saw that nigga Jon Boi's whip circling the block about two times. The nigga ain't from round here, and I remember that lil' beef y'all had recently."

"We squashed that shit, though," said Bang.

"Now when have you ever known any of them southside niggas squashin' beef wit' anybody? Think about it, big dawg. We took out one of theirs," Real One stated.

"But my mama, nigga?!" Bang growled.

"I'm just lettin' you know what I saw, Bang."

Bang tossed the phone back at Boodah and pulled the slide back on his pistol to chamber a round. He had blood in his eyes. What he was just told didn't make no sense to him. Because why would Jon Boi risk coming on his turf to off his mama? Because he sent his boys at one of his? Why didn't Jon Boi come for him?

A life for a life.

Then there was another thing to consider too. This bitch Moya. Everybody knows she and Tito were a vicious wrecking crew; even the cops should know this as well. Why would she show her face in the middle of a fresh murder investigation concerning her man at the possibility of being apprehended in the process?

Bang very much doubted Moya would take it this far with him when their minor differences earlier weren't even that fucking serious. Moya was the type to bring it to a nigga's chest if she had an issue.

Moya was a true standup bitch.

She was ruthless, though. Very unpredictable.

"What's the play, my nigga?" said TK.

Bang sneered. "Let's go see about this nigga Jon Boi. I want his muthafuckin' head!"

"What about Moya?"

"We'll cross that bridge when we get there," he said, and then fired up a Black & Mild. For a long time, Bang feared this day would come when his lifestyle would bring trouble where his mother lay her head.

But this was what he signed up for. There was no time for pity. You live by the gun, you die by the gun, and somebody was about to die today.

Chapter 9

It was soon about to be dark, and that didn't bother Moya, because that's when she really got her gangster shit on. She was fired up after killing Bang's mother, and now she craved more blood.

And now she had her lil' niggas with her. There were twelve of them young hyenas, always ready to blow a nigga's top back at her slightest whim. The death of Tito had them all itching to get out there and tear some shit up.

Tito had been their lieutenant and top enforcer. These were the silent assassins Tito had recruited, one of them being his very own godbrother. His murder hit Bizkit hard, so hard that he damn near blew his own brains out earlier.

Moya wanted to keep that one close to her.

Bizkit needed watching.

They were all strapping up, locking and loading for their mission to avenge Tito's death. Moya's only trap house was now the headquarters to get armored up. All of her youngins were dressing up in bulletproof vests, arming themselves with a selection of weaponry. They were preparing for war at its highest level.

"Y'all listen up!" Moya took the floor, and everybody in the house looked up at her. The faces that looked back at her were grim, saddened, and even happy to get on some gunplay shit. "Why are we here right now?" she asked.

"For war!"

"To represent for our man Tito!"

"To kill or be killed!" another said over the others, and that's the one who Moya asked to come up front. To her surprise, it was one of her favorites, Tyree, a young seventeen-year-old mutt that Tito found dumpster diving a year ago, having not eaten in three days. But today he was no longer a mutt; Tyree was a vicious young lion with a body count.

"Repeat what you said, Ty," said Moya.

"Kill or be killed!"

"What?"

Tyree repeated it.

"Louder!" She stood up on the sofa.

When Tyree shouted the four words, Moya told everybody in the room to do the same. Then, all of a sudden, they began to chant it, as Moya moved in rhythm with their voices like the tribes all did in harmony in the movie: *Black Panther*.

They made the whole house shake.

Then suddenly, there was a gunshot blast, and the whole room went quiet as they stared up at Moya clutching the chrome pistol in her hand. The look on her face was sinister as ever, her eyes blazing with a murderous glare.

"A moment of silence for Tito," she said.

Some bowed their heads, some looked up towards the ceiling. The rest just stared at Moya, ready for whatever she had to deliver.

"To kill or be killed," whispered Moya. "That means get out there and handle y'all's business," she said.

Her crew of shooters nodded.

"I ain't taking no more muthafuckin' losses! I wanna see each and every last one of y'all right here in this same room later. You got me?" she said.

Everybody responded in unison.

"I love y'all niggas," Moya told them. "Now let's go do the damn thang!" She raised her fist high.

At once, they gathered up their guns and other weapons and took it to the streets.

Later, in the all-black Yukon Denali lurking on the west side, Moya had Tyree, Bizkit, and young Flame in the back with the AR-15 laying across his lap. Moya made sure her youngins had the best firepower. All that bullshit that's known for jamming up in the middle of putting in work was not in their possession.

The whole truck was facing federal charges with all the steel they were carrying.

Moya's cellphone rang, and she checked the number. Lately, Toya and Joya had been blowing her phone up, but Moya would send them straight to voicemail every time. She knew they were aware of Tito's murder and were worried about her. She didn't want their sympathy right now; Moya wanted revenge and nothing more.

But the call wasn't from either one of them; it was one of her gunners calling.

"Talk to me," she replied.

"I got someone that wants to talk to you, Mo," said Baby G, the lil' nigga with the mad skills on the basketball court who Tito could never whip.

"Who?" she wanted to know.

"Me," came Naomi's voice, sending Moya sitting upright in her seat. "We need to talk, baby girl."

"You're here?" Moya perked up.

"Been here, Moya."

"Where?" she asked.

That's all she needed to know because there was no way she would deny her mother.

***

Patrick paced the floor of his father's study like a worried cat, as the professor himself stared at the silent phone sitting before him. They were waiting on a very important call that had yet to come.

"What the fuck!" Patrick blurted out, then resumed pacing.

The professor looked up at his son. "Calm yourself, Patrick. It'll come to us in a moment," he said.

"Calm? Dad, do you understand what this means? They are on us now, too close for comfort—or calmness! They killed Vinny and took Naomi. And here we both are like sitting ducks waiting to be slaughtered!" said Patrick.

"I very much doubt that."

"How come?"

That's when the professor hit a button on the mouse to activate the computer screen sitting on the desk in front of him. The screen showed six video feeds from the surveillance cameras surrounding the house. There was even a camera perched on top of the entrance gate twenty yards off the main entrance of the house. No one could enter through without their knowledge.

"We have a total of twelve armed sentries guarding the house as we speak. No one is coming through that gate without our permission."

"What if it's the Feds?" said Patrick.

The old man waved off the comment. "If the Feds were that close, we wouldn't be in this room right now."

"Right," said Patrick. "We'd be dead!"

"No, son. We would be halfway under the city, headed for our next destination," said the professor, giving his son that secretive look that spoke volumes. Patrick nodded, thinking about the underground tunnel his father had built years ago for emergency purposes like these.

The phone on the desk shrilled to life.

"Bingo," said Patrick.

In mid-reach, the old man had a premonition that something wasn't right. Slowly, he lifted the phone off its receiver. "Hello?"

"Are you ready for this, twin brother?"

The professor sucked in his breath and rose up out of the chair.

"Look out of your window, William," said Nicholas.

Instinctively, his gaze turned left to the large window overlooking the rose garden. The sun had just set across the horizon, but the sensor field lights surrounding the property illuminated the grounds clearly enough to see.

But he didn't see anything.

Then suddenly, the glass window shattered from a vicious blast, which no doubt came from a shotgun. The old man was struck in the stomach, sending him soaring backward onto the big oakwood desk. Behind him, his son Patrick cried out over the deafening gunfire as bullets penetrated his body, killing him.

And then the room fell silent.

Strewn across the top of his desk, the professor reached for his stomach and bellowed in pain. There was no blood; he hadn't been struck by a bullet, but by a bean bag from one of those riot control weapons.

As he pulled himself upright, the professor watched as several armed goons entered the room, circling him like a pack of wolves around a wounded doe.

"You killed my son," he hissed, reaching for the desk drawer where his gun was.

Another gunshot blast exploded, and the professor's hand suddenly became a mangled mess. He screamed in a bloodcurdling pitch that would give anyone chills.

"Just kill me!" the old man said. "Kill me!" he cried. He just wanted to die now, to get it over with.

He knew his brother was coming.

In his heart, he always knew his twin would show up and demand revenge for what he did. But it was what Nicholas had planned for him that scared him the most. We're talking about fifty years' worth of suffering.

Fifty years of pure hate.

The sound of a motorized vehicle approached from down the hall, as everyone present looked in its direction. The professor knew what that sound was; it meant trouble was coming.

And sure enough, it appeared in the office doorway a second later.

"Brother," said Nicholas, smiling across the room at the other image of him.

The professor swallowed nervously. "Nickie?"

The motorized wheelchair swerved into the room and crunched over shattered glass as it neared. For the first time in nearly fifty years, the two siblings were face to face.

"Do you know what this moment means to me right now?" said Nicholas.

"I'm sorry, Nickie," said his brother. "Forgive me! I was greedy. I let the money get to my head," he reasoned.

Nicholas just shook his head. "That won't work, brother."

"We can still..." the professor gasped the instant when, all of a sudden, Nicholas rose up out of the chair, causing even his men to do a double-take.

"We can never be anything but enemies," said Nicholas, drawing a knife as he stepped over Patrick's dead body and stalked toward his brother, then halted.

"Boss . . .?" said one of his goons, still dumbstruck.

"Everyone leave us be," the Italian ordered. "My twin brother and I have some unfinished business to take care of," he said without breaking eye contact with his twin.

No, the professor didn't want them to leave.

But they had no other choice. The boss said so.

***

The southside pool hall was jumping; everybody was out doing their thing and getting money as usual. But not Jon Boi, though—he was going through the motions. He stared blankly towards the front door of the pool hall, as his addled thoughts of his current situation caused him to worry.

His thoughts were on Moya.

He was in a bind.

Just now he had met with Chief of Police Calvin Butler about the murder of Moya Scott. The Chief wanted her dead, or else Jon Boi could kiss his own ass good-bye and do the rest of his life in prison. But for the past several weeks, Jon Boi had been stalling on the hit, saying that it was not that easy to get close to her. That he needed more time to strategize an inevitable plan.

That's why Moya kept bumping into him recently—it wasn't no coincidence at all. For three weeks now, Jon Boi had been getting closer and closer to executing his plan.

Every time he had a clear shot, he hesitated. His heart would not let him do it to her.

Four weeks ago, the Chief had set him up and taken him to jail on a bogus sales charge. Really, he was already blaming him for the murder of Jarrod Butler, the Chief's nephew, but Chief Butler couldn't pin the murder on him. So he had Jon Boi in custody after one of his do-boys planted an ounce of cocaine in his car. Chief Butler visited him while he was in the holding tank and told him what he really wanted. Why he wanted Moya dead, Jon Boi didn't know, but he damn sure wasn't trying to make it happen.

He was in love with Moya.

But what was he supposed to do? How in the hell could he get the Chief off his back?

Because tonight Chief Butler had met with him and given him twenty-four hours to have it done or go down. And taking a run for it was out of the question for Jon Boi. The last thing he wanted was to be on the run from the law when he could avoid it.

Or else he could murder the man himself, thought Jon Boi as he began to dwell on that. But the thought didn't get far when the doors suddenly burst open and niggas started running out of the pool hall.

"What's going on?" Jon Boi opened his door and got out. "Why is everybody runnin'?" he asked.

"There go Jon Boi right there!" someone shouted.

Instinct made Jon Boi reach for his pistol as a group of his homeboys ran towards him.

"You ain't heard?" asked Lil' Ron.

"Heard what?"

In the distance, gunshots sounded off, making them all look up in the direction of the gunshots.

"That's Bang and 'em!" said Lil' Ron's cousin.

"Bang?" Jon Boi paused.

"Yeah. They just shot up your crib!"

"What!" said Jon Boi. His baby mama was at the house!

And that's when shit got poppin'. "Oh no!" he cried out.

It was war.

Chapter 10

Zamon, Toya, Vonda, and Elijah were occupying Heather's front porch that evening as they waited for Moya to arrive. Joya was inside with the other women, including Heather's fiancé. They had awakened Avery Harris, who was dead tired after working twelve hours as a prison correctional officer. And now they had him all up in the mix.

While Elijah refused to leave Toya's side after realizing something tragic was in the midst, Zamon just wanted to get away from Vonda. She was shooting daggers at him with her eyes, and that shit made him very uncomfortable.

They shouldn't be around each other anyway, especially after messing around behind Joya's back. If she ever found out, shit was gonna get crucial.

Toya was saying something to Vonda about another situation when Moya pulled up on the scene. First her young shooters jumped out of the truck with their weapons in hand, then Moya herself got out and headed for the house. Walking alongside her was Bizkit, who had an AK-47 strapped across his shoulder and a pistol in his hand. Moya's presence had everybody at a standstill.

This was the first time Elijah had actually seen Moya in action after hearing so much about her.

But this was the other side of her that Toya had refused to tell him about.

"What the fuck are y'all doing out here like this?" Moya said the moment she reached the porch steps.

"Waitin' on your ass," said Vonda.

"Waitin' on me could get you killed," said Moya. "Don't you know it's a war out here nobody's safe from? Niggas is dying around this bitch, and y'all out here havin' a fuckin' family reunion." She frowned upon all of them.

"Mama needs to see you," Toya let her know right off, her arms folded across her chest.

"Where she at?"

"Inside."

"Then lead the way," said Moya, shooting everybody a look before turning to Bizkit. "You know what to do, my nigga," she told him. "Put Tron, Tyree, and Flame on post."

"I gotcha out here," he said.

"Love." She bumped fists with her soldier.

"Love."

Inside the house, the whole room went silent as Moya walked into the living room. The instant Naomi saw her daughter, she bolted from her seat and pulled Moya into her arms. Moya hurriedly stepped out of her mother's embrace; she was not the affectionate type.

Then Moya's phone rang.

It was one of her youngins calling from out there in the trenches.

"Talk to me," she answered.

"This me, Bojac," said the young shooter. "We got Wanky in the clutch right now. What you want me to do wit' his bitch ass?"

"What do you think, nigga?"

"Even under pressure he say he didn't do it."

"So what?" Moya met her mother's gaze. "Kill his ass anyway! No more phone action—just take care of business."

"Say no more," he said.

After she hung up, Moya stepped over to the arm of the sofa and sat down. She cast a glance across the room at Avery, and he shrugged his shoulders.

"Moya," said Naomi. "Let me speak to you in the kitchen for a minute."

With a deep breath, Moya got up and followed her mother into the big kitchen. Toya and Joya included themselves too, already knowing what the situation was about.

"Okay, Mama. Talk to me." Moya pulled up a chair.

"I met Nicholas Vontelli today," said Naomi, which got a surprised reaction from her daughter. "I know all about the hit on that reverend you took; I learned that from the professor himself today too."

"The professor?" Moya perked up at the mention of the Italian's name. "That's who sent for you, huh?"

"But that's not all, Moya," said Toya.

Moya was too occupied with the prospect of her mother meeting with both Italians today. She wondered how in the hell she pulled that off.

"Tito sold you out, baby," said Naomi.

"What!" Moya stiffened, her eyes staring up at her mother in puzzlement. "What did you just say, Mama?"

When Naomi began telling her about the visit with the professor and the evidence he provided against her, Moya looked on with a shocked expression. But when she described what had happened to Tito and what she witnessed with her very own eyes, Moya put her head in her hands and cried. This was the first time in ten years they'd seen her cry. But little did they know what those tears actually meant.

To make her cry was the worst thing ever.

She was genuinely hurt.

Tito betrayed her. He broke under pressure.

And that's when Moya broke . . . releasing that inner demon that had been fighting to be set free for a long time.

***

When his phone rang, Detective Shane Rogers was reluctant to pick it up and answer it. He already knew what it was about before he even spoke to anyone.

This was his peace time away from the department and those crucial streets. He was at home drinking a beer and watching *Bad Boys Forever* while his wife was laid out across the couch with her feet in his lap.

Rogers knew about the shootout between the southside and northside crews, but that wasn't his problem anymore. He was officially off duty, and that responsibility belonged to Detective Rachel Grant now. She was recently promoted to lieutenant and needed to get her hours in anyway.

Let her deal with fighting crime for tonight.

"So you're just gonna let it ring?" Pam asked, growing irritated by the annoying ringing of the phone.

"It'll stop in a second."

"But what if it's urgent?" she insisted.

He took another swig from his beer. Fuck it.

The ringing stopped.

"See." He rubbed her smooth feet, but now Pam was no longer in the same mood; her vibe was thrown off. She too sensed something was wrong and off about her husband not answering the phone—that wasn't like him at all.

Fifteen minutes later, there was a knock at the front door. Grudgingly, the detective got up with a fresh can of beer in his hand and went to answer it.

"We can't even watch the movie in peace," said Pam.

"Nope," he agreed. At the door, Rogers found two police officers standing before him, both wearing grave expressions.

"What can I do for you boys?" said Rogers.

"Chief Butler is dead, Lieutenant."

"Dead?" Rogers gasped. "What do you mean, dead?"

"Captain Brooks is asking for you, sir," the Bruno Mars–looking cop spoke up.

With a glance over his shoulder, he met his wife's gaze. The detective sighed and gave in to the force that beheld him.

Pam was not gonna like this; the chief's death was no doubt gonna do her in. Her best friend was his niece, and that was more trouble than Rogers needed.

Ten minutes later, he left his wife crying her eyes out as he raced to the murder scene.

If the city was on fire from the street war going on, the death of Chief Butler was about to turn it into lava. Every damn human being with a badge was about to retaliate, especially with Captain Marvin Brooks calling the shots now.

The chief lived out on Crawfordville Highway, alongside his two fellow officers, Henry McNiel and Susan Bostic, who were both on the scene when Rogers pulled up. On his way there, he was briefed by Detective Rachel Grant herself after making his first call to her. The chief had been in the kitchen when the murder took place; someone had dumped several rounds into him through the kitchen window while he was at the sink.

"It's a sad, sad moment for all of us," said Captain Brooks, who met Rogers at the front door and led him into the house past moving officers and the CSI team.

Rogers followed him through the house the chief had shared with his wife for twenty-one years before she passed three years ago.

The chief had two sons living out of state.

"I don't care how you do it, Shane," Brooks said as they turned into the kitchen doorway. "I want you to find the bastard that murdered my good friend. I know of your ties to the streets, so use all your resources to get me my man, or else find yourself out of a job!"

At the sight of the chief laid out on the kitchen floor with two bullets to his face and four more to his chest, the detective felt his knees go weak. He had to brace himself with a hand on the kitchen counter.

"Did you get Susan and Henry's statements?"

Brooks whirled around to face the detective. "Do you suspect them of playin' a part in this?"

"I'm just asking a question, Capt.," he said, noticing that the old man was ready to aim at anybody he could get for the murder of his friend. At that moment, Rogers could point the finger at anybody, and the captain would attack.

"This is your show then," said Brooks.

"What about Rachel?" he asked.

Captain Brooks balled up his face. "Fuck that two-timing bitch."

He snarled. "Look at my friend there, Shane!"

He looked down at the dead chief.

"Now get the fuck out of here and go find my killer," the old captain barked, pointing toward the front door.

And of course, Rogers did as he was told.

But where in the hell to look?

Who killed the chief?

"Rogers?" someone called out to him as he exited the house.

He looked up in the direction of the person and saw that it was Officer Susan Bostic headed his way. She was a tall, thickly built white woman with short blond hair. Susan was in a pair of fitted jeans and white Nike sneakers, her preferred attire while off duty. But she did have her service weapon on her hip, the detective noted.

"You got a minute?" she asked.

"Does it have anything to do with the murder?"

"It might," she said.

"What is it, then?" he asked, shoving his hands into his pant pockets, seeing a look in her eyes that made him uncomfortable.

"Not out here," she muttered.

"Where?"

She led him over to her home, which was behind the chief's house; she'd lived there for about six years now with her golden retriever, Betty. The same dog looked up at Rogers lazily from the front porch as he entered the house behind its owner.

"Okay, Sue. I'm listening," he finally replied.

"I saw Officer Matt Hollison and Hank heading over to the chief's place just before I heard the gunshots." She seemed very scared all of a sudden.

"What did you see, Sue?" he pressed.

"It's not what I saw, because I didn't see nothing, Shane. It's what I know," she told him.

"Then what do you know?"

She hesitated.

Rogers reached up and squeezed her shoulder, looking the woman dead in her eyes. "Was it Hank that did it?"

"I don't know, L.T.!" she sighed.

"Then tell me what the hell you fuckin' know, woman!" he growled at her, causing the woman to flinch in intimidation. Her hesitance was frustrating Rogers.

"Chief had Hank under extortion after he learned that Hank was on the payroll."

"Whose payroll?"

That's when she shivered. "Tito Shaw."

Now Rogers was really confused. And Tito was dead.

***

The professor stared into his brother's cold, hard eyes and knew that there would be no sparing him. In all their seventy years of living, who would have ever known it would come down to this?

Nicholas had been waiting a long time for this very moment—to finally confront his twin brother for betraying his trust.

Now here they were in full bloom.

"You had been faking it all these years, I see," the professor replied, thinking it was best to keep his brother talking to prolong the inevitable.

"I do not fake anything, William. Your pathetic plan to kill me almost worked; instead, I came out with two broken legs, a broken hipbone, and spinal injuries that had confined me to a wheelchair for multiple years. But through faith and the will to not be defeated, I found it very shocking too when it happened," said Nicholas.

"How much did you have to pay for that miracle?"

"Not as much as I'm about to make you pay," Nicholas sneered and lunged in for the attack. For a man of seventy, he was quite fast.

The professor moved to dodge the knife's long blade, but it still embedded itself into his right thigh. He screamed, and with his good hand, clasped his fingers over the metal stapler behind him on the desktop. With one lethal blow, he struck his brother across the head with it.

"Nice of you to fight back," Nicholas said with a wicked smirk, but the murderous glare in his eyes shone like headlights.

"Don't do this!" said the professor. He searched for something else to arm himself with besides a stapler. Two feet away was the drawer where he kept his gun; if only he could get to it in time.

Nicholas went in for the kill once again.

This time the professor reached out and blocked the next swipe of the knife's blade. Then with his injured hand, he desperately tried to shove Nicholas aside. Nicholas came up with the knife again and faked a strike toward his brother's midsection. The professor took the bait, and Nicholas drove the blade into his shoulder.

"Ahh! Muthafucker!" the professor roared and dazed Nicholas with a vicious elbow strike between the eyes. Then he shot out a hard hook to his jaw.

Nicholas said, "You're gonna have to do better than that!"

Suddenly, there was gunfire outside, but none of that meant anything to the twins. They were focused on one thing, and that was killing each other.

All hell was breaking loose outside.

As the professor went for the gun in the drawer, Nicholas pounced on him like a tick on a dog. He was jabbing his brother repeatedly with the knife this time, as the professor struggled to throw him off. He did everything he could to get Nicholas off him, but Nicholas was determined to finish him now.

But all that changed when Nicholas was suddenly pitched backward from an unexpected blast as a slug tore into his shoulder, putting him on his ass.

Bleeding from all over as he slumped against the side of the overturned throne chair behind the desk, the professor watched as multiple armed FBI agents swarmed into the room. He had never been so happy to see the Feds in his whole entire life.

"William 'The Professor' Vontelli," said Special Agent Larry Graham, coming into view as his men secured the area and sent for medical personnel. "I have a question for you."

The professor looked up at the man.

"Are you happy to see us?" Agent Graham asked.

"Help me," pleaded the professor.

"Oh, we got help coming. You just sit tight, old man. But I got somebody here I want you to see before we take your ass in," he said.

No reply.

But when another pair of legs stepped into his line of vision, the professor looked up into the face of their owner. He then gasped in unmistakable disbelief as he stared into the eyes of the last person he expected to see alive.

"Roland," he whispered. "I can't . . . believe it!"

And then everything went dark. But not for long.

Chapter 11

So much was going on that Jon Boi didn't know what to do next. After finding his crib shot the fuck up, he was relieved that Ashanti and his daughter were safe and sound. Bang had brought bullshit to his home and could have killed his family.

That was unacceptable.

Bang had to die tonight—no exceptions!

With twenty bands on his head, Jon Boi no doubt would see some results.

Jon Boi figured it had something to do with his mama being murdered earlier today. Someone must've seen him lurking on his turf, on Moya's trail, hours ago. Moya had been the one to cause Bang his pain, not him. Although he really wanted to—wished he should have taken it straight to Bang's chest when he had his chance.

Fuck the beef they were supposed to have squashed, Jon Boi was still planning on burning him anyway.

Then there was this other situation Jon Boi was faced with regarding the chief. He had had Officer Matt Hollison's wife and sons kidnapped tonight, making him go after the chief in order to get his family back alive. Hollison had been Jon Boi's credible resource on the payroll. He was the only person Jon Boi knew who could get close to the chief without causing suspicion.

What Jon Boi didn't know was that after tonight, Officer Hollison would no longer exist.

He was getting missing.

But he had yet to contact Jon Boi, letting him know the mission was already done. His family was still being held by them goons.

As he strolled through the dark city in an unmarked vehicle no one knew he was in, he thought about Moya and what she was doing, because he'd heard how her young shooters were out there setting it off in the streets. Right now, the streets looked like a ghost town—no, not even a police car was in sight.

The only ones out were them goons.

It was war time.

*** *

Jon Boi pulled up to a red light on Tennessee Street and spotted something going down up ahead at a local gas station. He recognized the all-blue Crown Vic belonging to that young nigga Remy, who was one of Moya's youngins, and he was being surrounded by four other niggas. Something in Jon Boi's mind told him to leave it alone, but his heart felt differently.

Whatever the situation was, he couldn't let these niggas team up on the little homie.

Jon Boi looked around him briefly, then he ran the red light and went to Remy's rescue.

As soon as he turned into the gas station's entrance, Jon Boi witnessed one of the niggas draw back and punch Remy in the face.

"What is it, yo!" Jon Boi got out the car and moved towards the group of niggas who had Remy hemmed up against the side of the car. In his hand, he clutched his Beretta but held it behind his back.

When the four niggas turned to face him, he was taken aback by what he saw.

All of them were Moya's young shooters.

Oh shit, Jon Boi thought to himself as he found himself intervening in the personal business between these five young goons. And Remy appeared to be in a bad position.

"What's up, Jon Boi?" said Spud.

"What the hell y'all got going on? You know it's bodies droppin' all around out there," he replied, releasing his grasp from his pistol. "Y'all right here on front street."

That's when Pooh, the leader of the pack and the same one who punched Remy, turned towards him with a grim expression.

"We know what's going on, big homie," he said. "But I got a muthafucker here who's scared to bust his gun."

"Who? Remy?" Jon Boi replied. "Not my lil' nigga."

"Yeah." Souljah shoved Remy back against the car. "Kill or be killed, nigga!" he said.

"Well," Jon Boi glanced at Remy. "I'm sure he has his reasons," he replied.

"Because he's a bitch!" said Spud.

Remy stepped up like he was hard now, his fists balled up ready to fight. "I ain't no bitch, nigga."

"You are a bitch!"

"Y'all chill the fuck out! It's too much shit going on right now for y'all to be out here clowning like this. If Moya knew y'all was out here like this, she would go the fuck off," said Jon Boi.

"Naw, Jon Boi," said Pooh. "If she knew this nigga didn't bust back when niggas was shootin' at us, you know what she'll do?"

"I know what she'll do."

That's when Pooh drew his pistol and put it to Remy's head. "She'll blow his muthafuckin' brains out," he hissed, glaring into Remy's eyes.

And that's exactly what she'll do too, thought Jon Boi as he regarded the young cat with silent pity. And this definitely wasn't the time to get on her bad side.

Speaking of which, Moya was in the kitchen getting herself together when gunshots rang out outside the house. Immediately, she bolted to her feet and rushed towards the front door with her pistol in hand.

"Everybody stay inside," she said.

"Moya!" Joya called after her, as Zamon rushed to her side. "Don't go out there! It's dangerous!"

But Moya didn't stop; she bolted out the door to go thug it out with Bang's men. Her shooters were going to war with them niggas. Both sides were shooting some big shit, as automatic rounds tore through some of her goons—and theirs too.

Moya upped her tool and went to dumping on them niggas as they tried to do a drive-by. But the truck had driven into an ambush, and now it was stuck.

Before long, Moya's side had won the gunfight, though two of her youngins were sprawled out on the concrete. She put her hands up to her head in anger as she stared down at her two dead homies.

"Pussy muthafuckaz!" Moya snapped and ran over to the Tahoe, which had crashed into a parked car at the curb. She snatched the passenger door open and stared into the truck at all four niggas, hoping she found at least one of them alive. "You killed my babies!" she said and shot one of the dead niggas in the head. They had killed Flame and Tyree.

"Moya?" Naomi said.

Moya looked at the nigga behind the wheel of the truck and shot him in the head too.

"Moya!" Naomi reached out a hand to touch Moya's shoulder, and Moya whirled around on her, aiming her pistol directly at her forehead.

"No!" Bizkit shouted as he ran up towards them. "Mo', stop! Stop!" he said.

Recognizing her mother, Moya lowered the pistol, and Naomi released a breath of relief. For a second there, she thought her daughter was gonna shoot her.

Young Tron came up alongside Moya, looking just as grim as she was, having lost two of his friends in the war just now. "We gotta bounce, Mo!"

Minutes later, Moya was back in the house with the others. Everybody looked at her now as a whole totally different person, having just witnessed her in true form outside.

"I can't have you here, Mama. It's too dangerous," said Moya, looking at her twins next. "Both of y'all go wit' Mama back home. I don't wanna hear no excuses—I need y'all out of this city tonight!"

"I can't leave, Moya!" her twin said.

"You got no choice, Toya."

"No. I got a job . . ." Toya said.

"What's more important to you, Toya, your job or your fuckin' life?"

"Those children," said Toya. "Desiree."

That shut Moya's mouth up.

Heather then stepped up, agreeing with Moya, knowing exactly what she meant. Toya wasn't trying to hear that shit, and so Moya intervened.

Moya stepped up into her twin's face and scowled into her eyes, her heart no longer with feeling. "You're gonna do as I say, twin."

"Fuck that, Moya, you're the reason why any of this mess is happening. It's your fault those boys out there are dead—" Toya was too slow to prevent Moya from wrapping her hand around her throat in a vise grip.

"Bitch, who you talkin' to?"

"Let her go." Elijah reached for Moya.

And that's when Bizkit drew his pistol and put it to his head. "You touch her, and you're dead."

Elijah held his hands up.

"Let her go, Moya." Naomi stepped in between her two daughters, grabbing Moya's arm. "That's your twin. We don't need to go through this shit. Let her go."

"Please, twin," Joya said, seeing how red Toya's face was getting, and her eyes were bulging out.

Moya let her go. "You're lucky you're my twin."

"We'll leave tonight," said Naomi. "That's an order."

"But what about Mama?" said Heather.

"We're all going," said Naomi. "No exceptions."

***

Desiree was up watching cartoons and eating Jell-O while Ella Mae slept on the other bed next to hers. The old lady was exhausted. Desiree couldn't have asked for a better caregiver, because Ella Mae didn't crowd her space or have to pretend with her.

But Desiree missed her friends like crazy. She wondered if Alexis and Jamaal were up this late watching TV and eating junk food. Maybe tomorrow she could get Toya or somebody to bring them up to visit her.

That would be good.

Yesterday, Toya brought her a greeting card with all of the students in her class's signatures on it. Receiving that card made her feel special.

Desiree was then distracted from her thoughts when she heard someone screaming. It sounded like it was just outside the door, and she peered over at the old lady, finding her still asleep. The commotion didn't wake her up, but it did make Desiree curious about what was going on.

She wanted to go see.

This wasn't the first time she'd thought about getting down from the bed and taking a journey. So she put her thoughts into action and silently climbed down from the bed. It was a painful task, but she completed the mission.

Another cautious glance over at Ella Mae encouraged Desiree to keep moving. She was knocked out cold and snoring softly in the bed.

She'd probably be out till morning.

Desiree padded across the floor in her hospital socks and slipped quietly out the door.

By this time, the screaming had ceased, but Desiree was already on the move. To her surprise, she saw another young kid out in the hallway—a white boy who appeared to be no older than her. He was rolling around in a wheelchair, with one of his legs encased in a cast. The boy looked up, spotted her, and gave her what she assumed was a curious look.

"Who are you?" the little blond-haired boy asked.

"Who are you?" she shot back.

"I'm Josh."

"What happened to you, Josh?"

He glanced down at his broken leg. "I fell from my treehouse," he said. "I was climbing up and missed a step. What're you doing here?"

"I broke my ribs."

Josh gave her a skeptical look. Something in his eyes told her that he didn't believe her.

"What?" She felt offended by his expression.

"I heard the doctors talkin'," he said. "You're the girl whose father pushed her down the stairs?"

"Why do you wanna know?" she frowned.

"Because." Josh paused. "I think he's a jerk!"

"He's a coward for pickin' on me."

"He's a punk."

"He's a bitch!"

"He's a total asshole!" said Josh.

And Desiree liked him already.

"You have pretty eyes," he told her, and that was all it took to make her smile.

Now she really liked him.

For the next twenty minutes, they talked and laughed about anything and everything. In the process, some of the night-shift medical staff watched them curiously and with envy, wishing they could be as carefree while they dealt with all the bullshit and constant frustrations.

"Who was that screaming out here earlier?" asked Desiree.

"Some kid who got shot in his legs."

"Black kid?" she wondered.

Josh nodded. "Wanna go check it out?"

"You know where they took him?"

"No," he said, "but I know which way he was taken."

You didn't have to tell her twice; Desiree was down with it. They began their search for the kid who was shot. Desiree knew she couldn't be gone long, just in case Ella Mae woke up and found her missing.

As they continued their mission, Desiree turned into the path of a man headed in the direction from which she had come. She looked up at the stranger as he passed, and he gave her an interesting glance. She would have sworn she knew this man.

He seemed so oddly familiar.

But she proceeded on with her journey, not knowing the person she had just laid eyes on would change her life.

***

Officer Henry McNiel, aka Hank, was seething mad as he leaned against the side of his Ford F-250 truck, watching the activity transpiring next door. He couldn't believe the chief had been killed under his watch.

He had just spoken with him an hour ago.

And that's when Hank began to recollect his thought process during the last time he remembered seeing Chief Butler alive. He had just finished shaving when he heard a pickup truck turn into the gravel driveway from the highway. He looked out the window and saw that the truck belonged to Matt Hollison. Matt was his buddy, so he went out to the porch to meet him.

But instead of turning into his driveway, which he and the chief shared, Matt parked his truck in front of the chief's house.

That still didn't stop Hank from saying hello.

The instant Hank saw Matt's face, he immediately figured something was wrong. After he questioned Matt about his behavior, Matt told him that he was having trouble at home with the wife. That he sought after the chief's wisdom and lending ear. Both men approached the house, the chief let them inside, and they had a long talk about love and marriage.

Then Matt left, fifteen minutes before Hank heard the gunshot and came running. By the time he reached the chief's house and found him dead, the killer was gone.

Hank summoned Susan, who too came running with her gun in hand. But there was nothing they could have done for the chief except for calling it in.

Now, as Hank dwelled on the situation, he still found it odd that Matt had driven all the way out to see the chief. Of all the years he and the chief had been living next to each other, he had never seen Matt come over—not even during the cookouts and get-togethers.

Hank sensed foul play was amiss on Matt's behalf. He also remembered the guy's shifty eyes and overly anxious manner to leave the house when the chief offered to pour them all another glass of scotch. Matt was a scotch guy, and for him to decline a second drink was questionable on his part.

Could Matt be involved in the chief's murder? If so, then why would he want the chief dead?

Another thought came to mind, and Hank wondered if the chief was applying pressure on Matt for any reason, and Matt used the wife troubles to throw him off.

There was only one way to find out, and that was to confront the man himself.

Hank locked the house up and hopped in his truck to go take that drive. As he was leaving, Hank noticed Susan and Detective Shane Rogers exiting from her house. They looked in his direction, Rogers raised his hand at him, and Hank turned away and drove on.

Once on the road, he decided to phone Matt in advance but got no answer. So he headed straight for the officer's house, where he figured Matt would be.

Matt lived out on Capitol Circle near the airport. When he reached the cop's residence, Hank saw two vehicles parked in the driveway. But it was the pickup truck that was left with its driver's door halfway open and the dome light on inside the cabin. Hank got out and approached the truck, only to find it empty. He then turned for the house after shutting the door to the truck.

To his surprise, he found the front door hanging off one of its hinges as though it had been kicked in. That alone was probable cause for Hank to draw his weapon.

"Matt? It's me, Hank," he called out into the house before toeing the front door open wider with his boot. "Matt? Are you in there? Cynthia? Anybody home?"

No answer.

The house was quiet except for the TV in the living room, playing an old episode of Modern Family.

With his gun up and ready, Hank entered the house and eased down the corridor into the family room. No one was there. He moved on towards the kitchen and found it still set up as though the family was having supper and had suddenly abandoned it for some reason.

"Matt?" Hank called out again as he exited the kitchen for the hallway leading towards the back of the house. And that's where he found Matt Hollison, sitting on the floor of his sons' bedroom with his pistol clutched in his hand.

"What are you doing, Matt?"

"He took my family, Hank," Matt cried like a baby, leaning against a dresser mounted with soccer trophies and toy race cars. "He made me do it!" he said.

"He who, Matt? Put the gun down, buddy. Who made you do what?" Hank spoke calmly, easing into the room.

Matt said, "I didn't wanna kill the chief. He was my idol. But he said he would kill my family—"

When Hank saw him place the gun to the side of his head, he panicked.

"Stop! No, Matt! Talk to me, buddy. Look at me," Hank replied, setting his gun down on top of the dresser at his left. "I'm not here to harm you. I want to help you! Please, let me help," he pleaded.

"It's too late," said Matt, and he closed his eyes.

"Matt, no!" Hank lunged for him.

Boom!

There was nothing else to talk about.

Chapter 12

His name was Clyde Summers, and he worked for the county's morgue. For more than thirty-five years, Clyde had been operating on dead bodies, preparing them for burial after the coroners were done with them. He had a quiet, nasty, complicated job, but over the years, he'd become accustomed to the stench of death. Hell, it paid the bills, too.

But tonight he was stacked with bodies; he had at least eleven he hadn't gotten around to yet.

"Must be one helluva night out there, huh?" he whispered as he leaned in close to an elderly woman's corpse, stitching her lips shut.

"You talk to the dead too, huh?" a voice replied.

Startled from his task, Clyde looked up from the operation table towards the door. And there stood Moya, dressed in all black, with armed goons behind her.

"You can't be in here!" said Clyde, pulling a sheet over the exposed face of the dead woman.

"I can be wherever the fuck I wanna be, nigga," she replied as she entered the room.

The temperature seemed to have dropped a lot more with her presence, giving the already refrigerated atmosphere in the room a darker chill.

"I'm lookin' for Tito Shaw. You seen him?"

"Who?" the man said.

Moya snapped her fingers, and instantly her two men began to uncover the bodies on the line of corpses circling the cool room. They were snatching sheets off all of them.

"What's the meaning of this intrusion?" said Clyde, his voice loud and shaky. He came around the operating table at once, and Moya didn't even budge.

"Oh. There goes J-Rock's bitch ass!" said Moya, noticing one of the uncovered bodies.

Clyde shivered with outrage, having been intruded upon and treated disrespectfully in his sanctuary.

"Right here!" said Bizkit.

"Oh yeah?" Moya perked up and drew her pistol finally, making her way across the room. Tito's body had been the one next in line to be operated on.

Both Bizkit and Tron stepped back, away from the body, to give Moya her space. Then Tron pulled up his assault rifle and aimed it at Clyde, who was standing there watching Moya in silent forlorn.

When Moya approached Tito's body, she stood there glaring down at him for a long, silent moment. At first, something in her chest moved at the sight of him; then she suddenly felt a sense of giddiness wash over her. Then that demon came out of her.

Blocka!

One shot to the head, right there between the eyes, made her want to do it again.

"I gave you everything, nigga!" she said, and shot him again in the face. "You hurt me, muthafucka! You bitch-ass nigga, I loved you like a brother!" Moya balled up her fist and punched Tito's dead corpse in the mouth.

"Please, stop it," said Clyde.

Bizkit dropped him with a jab to the mouth, as Tron now stood over him with a menacing glare.

"You broke my heart, Tito," she sneered, stepping over to the operating table to take up an already bloody surgical knife Clyde had recently used. "Now I'ma take yours."

The man prayed for mercy as he watched Moya carve Tito's heart out of his chest. It took her a very difficult time to do it, but she succeeded.

"I always wanted to do some shit like that," Moya said as she held Tito's heart in her hand.

Tron looked a little sick to his stomach.

There was blood all over the place as they looked at Moya, realizing just how insane her ass really was. The bitch had literally cut the nigga's heart out and now held it up in the air like a Super Bowl trophy.

127

"Guess what this is, y'all?" she said.

No one answered.

"The heart of a pussy nigga I thought was my main man!" she said. Then she dropped the heart on the floor and stomped on it. "Not no more it ain't."

***

Ella Mae was still knocked out cold when the door to the room opened, and a body slid inside and closed it shut behind it. Then the intruder approached the bed where the old lady slept and reached out a hand to her.

"No!" came Desiree's cry, as she rushed into the room and charged at the man standing over the bed. "Leave her alone!"

Ella Mae's eyes fluttered open instantly at the sound of a man's agonizing howl that made her panic.

There was a tussling commotion going on in the dark room, and the old lady switched on the lights.

"Oh my God!" Ella Mae cried.

Like a little rag doll, the man held Desiree up in the air by her gown as she squirmed in his grasp, punching and clawing at his thick, muscled forearms. In his hand was a blood-dripping scalpel, and he was bleeding profusely from his side where Desiree had stabbed him twice.

"Mama," said Roland, looking from the old lady to the girl. "Tell her to quit fightin' me."

"Put that child down right this second!" Ella Mae scrambled out of the bed and rushed over to her son to take the frantic girl away.

Roland said, "You can have her."

Then the old lady, with Desiree in her embrace, scurried over to the corner of the room, away from him. Seeing the fear in his mother's eyes made Roland feel really uncomfortable. But he was badly injured, which made him toss the knife down and rip his shirt away to examine his wounds.

"Who is that man?" whispered Desiree.

As soon as the shirt came off, Ella Mae zoomed in on the two bullet wounds that marked their entry along his upper torso. It was then that Ella Mae knew her mind wasn't playing tricks on her. She was looking at her very own son, Roland.

He was back from the dead.

"That's my baby," said the old lady, setting Desiree aside and rising to her feet.

Desiree looked on in silent confusion as she watched the old lady make her way over to the bleeding stranger and fuss over his injuries.

"You need to let a doctor look at this," said Ella Mae. "You're gonna need stitches, Roland."

He then glared over at Desiree, and she glared back, now recognizing him as the same man she'd passed by in the hallway earlier.

"You stay put," Ella Mae told the girl as her injured ribs began to throb in agony. So she climbed up in bed and lay down.

"You got some explaining to do, son," Ella Mae told Roland once they had made it to the ER and were now waiting to be stitched up.

She couldn't tear her eyes away from her son, seeing how much he'd changed over the years. He was forty years old now, stockier in stature, and still handsome as ever. Ella Mae was fighting the urge to wrap her arms around him but didn't want to hurt him further. Then again, the thought was intriguing.

"I had to, Mama," he said.

"You had to, why?"

"Because I was still under the FBI's protection. Part of my federal sentence was to lead them into capturing my drug connect. But then things got out of hand to the point I had to protect myself," he said. Then he told her how the bullet-proof vest had nearly saved his life, although two rounds had indeed penetrated his shoulder and collarbone area. "The Feds took me in and put me away under protective custody."

"But why so long?" she asked.

"That's how long it took for them to find him," he said. "Because after he sent those boys to kill me, he went deep underground where he couldn't be found."

Ella Mae said, "But you've been around all this time since then?" She was referring to him being in Florida.

"I was in New Jersey."

"New Jersey? What's way up there?"

Before he could answer, the doctor came into the room to perform his duty.

She left to go be with Desiree, and boy did she have some questions for her. The girl fired so many questions at her that Ella Mae was having a hard time answering them fast enough.

"So is he here to stay now?" she asked.

"I sure hope so," Ella Mae sighed.

The girl muddled over that for a moment.

"I hope Ms. Scott don't give me an 'F' now."

"Why would she do that?"

Desiree looked up into her eyes. "For hurtin' her daddy," she said.

"She won't."

"How do you know?"

"How do you know?"

"Because," Ella Mae said, "You were protectin' me."

***

Before heading out, Joya needed to stop by the apartment to grab a few things. Toya was still in her feelings about her and Moya's earlier confrontation.

Naomi just wanted to get back to Jacksonville, but her heart didn't want to leave without Moya. She knew Moya would not see things her way now, especially after what went down back at the house. Moya was beyond reasoning when her reputation was on the line.

So Naomi was forced to basically put her trust in her daughter's shooters and Moya's ability to stand firm against whatever came her way. Moya was proven worthy to rule the streets under her command, so Naomi had to respect her position.

She had to suck it up and keep hope alive.

When they made it to the apartment, both twins went inside while Naomi stayed behind. She wanted to keep her eyes open and alert.

"I can come if you want me to," said Zamon. "I don't have nothing left here anyway."

"Where is your family, Zamon?" she asked.

Zamon leaned against the trunk of the car next to her, thumping out a Newport cigarette to smoke. "My people are originally from Cairo, Georgia. I grew up down in Quincy with my uncle Byron and my brotha Willie. I burned my bridges with my uncle, and Willie's in prison."

"How did you burn your bridges?"

"Being in the streets." Zamon readjusted the gun at his waist.

"But what did you do, Zamon? Don't try to pull the wool over my eyes. I'm not one of those naive girls you've been dealing with," she said.

"Girls? I only deal with your daughter."

"And Vonda," she replied, looking at him sternly. "I'm not stupid; I see how y'all look at each other."

Zamon didn't respond.

"Loyalty means everything to me, Zamon. And the only reason why we're talkin' right now is because I feel I can talk some sense into you." Naomi paused for effect. "And neither are my daughter—both of y'all are with the bullshit. Why be with each other and can't stay true to one another?"

"I love Joya," he declared.

"But you have a tender dick you can't control," she told him straight up like it is. "And what I know about tender dick individuals is that they eventually cause themselves to wish they never even had a dick. You understand where I'm coming from, Zamon?"

"I understand."

"You better, or else you're gonna find yourself without one," she said. "Because I'll cut that fucker off myself before I let your weak-mindedness be the cause that my daughter catches something she can't have cured."

With that said, Naomi moved away from him, stepping between two cars parked outside the apartment building. She then made her way towards the twins' apartment and let herself in like she did earlier that day.

The moment she walked into the apartment, she heard Toya in her bedroom arguing with Elijah.

"He wants her to go stay with him instead," said Joya, appearing in the kitchen doorway with her travel bag. A second ago, she had received a call from Lance Winters informing her that the quarter million dollars she demanded of him was now in a secure offshore account.

"Toya's coming with us," Naomi said. Then she yelled for her to tighten up. "I don't got all night, Toya!"

A minute later, both Toya and Elijah exited the room. Elijah then kissed her on the lips and brushed past Joya and her mother, heading for the door.

"I can't deal with this mess," said Toya, after she heard Elijah's car roaring away outside.

"Let's go." Naomi helped Toya with her bags and turned for the door.

Outside, the women saw Zamon conferring with two other guys who looked up at them as they descended the stairs.

"Peanut!" said Toya. This was her and the twins' cousin from Roland's side of the family. It was his baby mama Tanya who had taken her girl Moya in earlier after almost killing that chump Brodrick.

"What it do, cuz?" said Peanut, then he regarded Naomi with obvious wonderment as she approached. "I thought I'd never see you again. Mama was just talkin' about you recently, saying how she missed how y'all used to give them hell back in the day."

"How is Emma doing anyway?"

"Still the same ol' Emma, talkin' shit and dippin' snuff, and gettin' on my goddamn nerves," he said.

"Well, tell her I said hey." Naomi opened Joya's car door and tossed the bag onto the backseat.

"Where y'all headed?"

"To Jacksonville," said Joya.

"Smart move," said Peanut. "Anywhere is better than here right now. It's a war out there, and them crackaz are snatchin' niggas up left and right. Especially after somebody done fucked around and killed the chief of police."

"Chief Butler?" Toya gasped.

Joya did too. "Whaaat?!" she said with surprise.

"It's crazy out there," said Peanut.

When everything was said and done, the females got into the car while Zamon stood by looking crazy. Naomi then glanced out the window at him and saw the pathetic look he had on his face.

"Boy, get in the car with your tender dick ass!" she rolled down the window and said to him.

You didn't have to tell him twice. Zamon hopped in the back with Toya, and they were on their way, getting the hell out of Tallahassee until the smoke clears.

If it ever does clear.

Who knows!

Chapter 13

The night went by in a flash, and before he even knew it, morning was present and another day had begun. And still, Detective Shane Rogers was scratching his head in confusion. Here it was, they'd found out who the chief's killer was and still couldn't get him. The muthafucker had shot Hank and ran for it, placing himself as one of America's most wanted men, considered armed and dangerous.

The crazy thing about it all was the fact that his family was set free when he thought they had been killed. Now his wife was left to raise two badass kids on her own. The whole department was in a terrible frenzy over the fact that Matt Hollison had murdered two of their own and still got away.

Captain Brooks was about to have a damn stroke.

Everybody was affected by the incident.

From one crime scene to another, and another, and a fourth one throughout the course of the night had Rogers dizzy with paperwork. Pam had to bring him coffee and breakfast to the station. The man was swamped in murder investigations and had only solved two of them.

One of Moya's young goons was said to probably have been involved in some of the killings throughout the night. He was now suffering gunshot wounds in both of his legs, after being dumped outside the Emergency Room entrance last night. Authorities suspected his own people had shot him, and now they were leaning heavily on him.

But the little bastard refused to say a peep.

If only Rogers could get him to talk, then maybe he could speed up the process on solving some of these cases. There had been times when he'd broken some of the toughest niggas in the streets. Now he had this young kid who went by the name Remy, and he couldn't even get him to budge.

Detective Rogers was beginning to doubt his ability to uphold that respected reputation he had built for himself over the years. He had his younger colleagues watching, and they were not satisfied with his performance.

Was he losing his touch? Was it time for him to hang it up now after thirty-two years behind the badge?

Blood, sweat, and tears—he'd endured his whole entire journey working as a cop. It was about that time to retire and be rid of all this mess.

"Lt.?" someone pulled him away from his thoughts. Rogers looked up and saw Detective Philis Martin peeping her big square head into his office.

"What is it, Philis?" he frowned. Rogers wanted to go home and crash; he was dead tired and frustrated.

The multi-racial woman detective slipped into the office and shut the door behind her. This was one of Rogers' favorite detectives; she was articulate and very open-minded. Her first month on the job she'd helped solve a double-homicide, and that was an A-plus in Rogers' book.

"You won't believe who I saw leavin' TMH just now after interviewing a couple of witnesses on the liquor store shootin'."

"Who?" he asked.

"Roland Scott," she said.

"Roland Scott?" thought the detective, rolling the name around in his memory bank. And just when Philis opened her mouth to continue, he pushed back in his chair and looked at her intensely. "Roland Scott is dead, Philis."

"No," she said, sliding her cellphone across the desk for him to see with his own eyes. "He is very much alive."

"How can this be possible?" he whispered.

"Anything's possible."

As he stared down at the phone's screen, Detective Rogers began to experience some dark, troubling visions. He was looking at Roland Scott in the flesh, for he would never forget that face. Philis had captured his photo almost up close and personal, just as he was waiting at the curb outside the hospital for a taxicab.

Years ago, Roland had saved his life. After chasing a suspect into an alley and being gunned down by that same suspect, it was Roland who had come to his rescue. How could he ever forget the man who saved his life?

"I know you can get the scoop on this one," said Philis. The only reason she remembered Roland's face was because they both had gone to school together, and he was one of the few boys she'd really wanted to get with.

"I would like to hear that one," he told her.

"Didn't they have his funeral like ten years ago?" she said.

"I was there," he admitted.

"Really?"

"Yeah," he said. "Roland's the reason I'm still alive right now." Then he deleted the photo from her phone and excused her from his office. Rogers closed his eyes and leaned back in his seat, wondering what in the hell was going on.

The father of one of Tallahassee's most feared women was back from the dead.

Did Moya know? he wondered.

Maybe Roland's presence could change things now; maybe he could talk some sense into his daughter.

***

It was 9:00 in the morning, and Moya had her right leg cocked up on the front passenger seat, getting head from a young hustler. She had the nigga sucking on her clit hard as she grabbed the back of his head, mushing his face between her legs. In her other hand, she clutched a sizzling blunt of Loud, getting high while she got her rocks off.

Then she busted her nut, coming all in his mouth, making sure he drank every single drop.

"You did your thang, boo," said Moya, pulling up her basketball shorts before tossing the nigga an ounce of dope for his services. "Now get the fuck out my face!"

Outside the car stood four of her shooters, all of them strapped and guarding her existence.

After situating herself, Moya got out of the car and took a pull from her blunt. She was at her spot where Roland had once operated a car detailing shop, but now it was a weed dispensary she owned. Ever since it became legal in Florida, she was one of the first business owners to open up a shop in the city.

And the business was booming good.

They all were posted up behind the building, having been summoned there by Moya. She wanted all of her goons present and not a soul late.

Moya had something on her mind, and she wanted to bring it to the attention of her crew.

"Who in the fuck shot Remy last night?" she demanded.

Hesitantly, Pooh stepped forward, and Moya wasn't surprised to see that it was him.

"Mind tellin' me why you did it, Pooh?"

"Because that nigga was scared to bust his gun," he explained, going into detail about what had gone down the night before.

Some of the others who were involved in the incident added their two cents.

"Did I ask any of you muthafuckas to say something?" she snapped, throwing the butt of her blunt down and drawing her gun from her shoulder holster. "The next one speak out of turn gettin' bust! Test me if you think I'm playin'."

No one was willing to test her.

Then Moya marched over to Pooh and put her gun to his temple.

"This is what you should have done to Remy."

"I did," said Pooh nervously.

"Then why didn't you bust your gun and kill his ass for not takin' care of his business?"

Pooh swallowed. "I shot him in the legs to teach him a lesson," he said.

"To teach him a lesson?"

He nodded.

"Bang!" Moya screamed in his face, and Pooh flinched—and that was the wrong thing to do. She then stepped back a few feet and shook her head at him. "I got a lesson for you now, Pooh, since you like giving out lessons," she said coldly.

It was then that Pooh knew he was doomed.

"Ray Ray, Bizkit, Animal, Lil Petey. Beat this nigga's ass to sleep!" she commanded.

On command, all four youngins rushed Pooh at once and latched onto his ass like a bunch of leeches. And they were doing Pooh dirty, beating him with beer bottles, a pipe, fists, and feet. To her satisfaction, Pooh fought back as hard as he could.

The others watched silently, doing their best to remain humble about it.

"If he hit that ground, stomp his ass," Moya said. Then her cellphone rang. Moya reached into the pocket of her shorts for the phone. "Hello?" she answered, never taking her eyes away from the beatdown.

And then Pooh fell to the ground.

"Hey, Mo," said Desiree in a joyful voice.

"What's up, Dez?" she perked up.

"Will you come to the hospital? I need to talk to you," the girl said.

"About what, boo? Are you okay?"

"No."

"What's wrong?"

"Come here, and I'll tell you. Ella Mae says I can't talk about it over the phone. Are you coming?" Desiree wanted to know.

"You know I'm coming," said Moya. Then she promised the girl she would be there in a minute. "I got something I need to do first."

"Okay," said Desiree.

Moya hung up the phone and turned her attention back to the physical action. Pooh was still on the ground and barely moving, and her four goons were still giving his ass the business.

"That's enough," she said.

They then backed away from Pooh's body, which was bloody and bruised. Pooh wasn't moving, and Moya wondered if he was still alive.

She stepped over, knelt down near his head, and nudged his shoulder.

He was still alive but unconscious.

"Hope you learned your lesson, Pooh." She rose up and faced the rest of her crew. She eyed them all with a hard look. "The next muthafucka step out of line and this is what you'll get. Bizkit?"

"Yeah?" he answered.

"Kill that muthafucka!" she said as she made her way back toward her car. Then she got inside and headed for the hospital.

***

Club Flavors was the number one strip club in all of North Florida, located right off Highway 90 in the Midway, Florida area. Flavors had won two consecutive years, topping even Miami's K.O.D. and putting Midway, Florida on the map. And Dough Murphy, the owner of the extravagant strip joint, had worked his fingers to the bone to reach these new heights.

He was the man now, with some of the baddest women in the world of dancing, and was swimming in money.

It took him ten years to do it. Ten years after Roland had left him with over a hundred fifty grand he owed him before his untimely death. So instead of fucking over the money, he decided to build himself a club.

Doughboy was living the high life.

He was hood rich.

A bitch can't tell him nothing now, because he was officially out the game and making honest money from his business. Okay, well, not that honest, but he wasn't selling dope anymore.

Then the telephone sitting on his big corporate desk rang, interrupting him from counting his money.

"Get that, Sugah!" he said, a cigarette dangling from his mouth as he fed bills into the money counter machine.

Sugah, a thick redbone bitch who reminded you of that hoe Roxy from Players Club, reached to answer the phone. She was butt-ass naked, sitting across from Doughboy, with the huge wall safe standing open behind him.

"Hello? Club Flavors, this is Sugah speaking," she replied in her business voice, her Puerto Rican accent giving it a hint of seductiveness.

"Tell Doughboy this is Roland," said Roland.

"It's Roland," Sugah said, extending the phone toward him as she laid eyes on the money pile sitting in front of her.

"Roland?" Doughboy looked up.

Sugah gave him an impatient look, still holding the phone out to him.

He snatched the phone away from her, and then she stuffed another two twenty-dollar bills up her pussy. By now she had about four hundred dollars up there.

"Who the hell is this on my phone?"

"It's me, cuz. Come open the back door and let me in," said Roland.

At the sound of his voice, Doughboy bolted up to his feet, his eyes staring directly at the secured office door. There was no way this was Roland. He was dead.

"I don't got all day, Antonio," added Roland, knowing that would get his cousin moving if nothing else. Doughboy used to hate when Roland called him by his first name.

And that's what did it, causing Doughboy to hurry for the door and tear up out of there.

"Sheeit!" Sugah muttered as she looked back over her shoulder, then back at all the money on the desk. Then up into the wall safe where the real money was.

In three seconds flat, she snatched two stacks of bundled bills from the safe and headed out the door. By the time Doughboy got back, the money would already be hidden, and she would be right back where he left her.

And sure enough, that's exactly what happened. Then Doughboy told her to get out while he talked privately with his visitor. There was a worried look on his face as he reclaimed his seat behind the desk. Sugah looked from him to the big, muscle-bound, handsome-ass nigga she suspected to be Roland.

"Out, Sugah!" barked Doughboy.

"Okay, Daddy!" She shimmied the hell up out of there, ass bouncing all over the place and titties jumping like crazy. But she did make a point of squeezing Roland's dick on her way out the door, giving him a throaty response.

Roland slammed the door shut and locked it.

"Is that your top bitch?" Roland asked. "The one you got counting your money with you?"

"That's my top bitch and personal assistant."

With a shake of his head, Roland leaned forward to pick something up from the floor. Then he tossed it at Doughboy, hitting him in the chest with it. It was a crumpled-up twenty-dollar bill dampened with pussy juice.

"You need to pick better help around your money, or your ass gonna end up broke," said Roland.

Doughboy tucked the money in his shirt pocket, making a note to beat that bitch's ass later.

"Now," Roland replied as he pulled up a chair to have a seat. "Go ahead and ask, cuz."

"How did you do it?" Doughboy didn't even hesitate.

Roland figured that would be the first question. Shit, of all the people he'd reunited with so far, they all had asked that same question.

"If I tell you, then I'll have to kill you," he said with a straight face.

"Okay. Why, then?" he asked next.

"Why didn't you give Naomi the money you owed me when you heard that I was dead?"

Doughboy couldn't even answer the question.

"My point exactly," Roland said with a shrug, then he took one of his cigarettes out of the pack on top of the desk.

"You seen Naomi yet?" Doughboy asked.

"No."

"What about Joya and Toya?"

"Not yet," Roland admitted, wishing he had already.

"But you've heard, though, right?"

He held his cousin's gaze for a moment as the cigarette smoke swirled up around his face.

"Heard what, cuz?" he said.

"About Moya."

"What about her?" said Roland.

All Doughboy could do was shake his head, then he told his cousin everything he knew.

Chapter 14

At the sound of a door slamming shut, Zamon turned over in bed just in time as Joya snatched the towel away and climbed in bed with him.

"Mama just left, so we got enough time to fuck," said Joya, ripping down his boxers to expose his semi-hard morning dick.

"Damn, that muthafucker look scrumptious!"

"What about Toya?" he asked.

"She's gone too," said Joya, positioning her pussy over his face in a sixty-nine position. "Stick two fingers in my ass while you eat my pussy," she moaned.

How could he deny that?

She was fresh out the shower, and that pussy smelled like apple cinnamon.

"That's what the fuck I'm talkin' about," Joya said when he obliged her desires, then stuffed his hard dick back into her hungry mouth.

For the next hour they sucked and fucked all over the guest room Naomi had made him sleep in the night before. Boyfriend or not, she wasn't going for him and Joya sleeping in the same bed together.

"It's shopping time for you," said Joya once they were done getting freaky. "You need some clothes and stuff to wear. You know I can't have my man not lookin' bossed up!"

"I can dig it," he said.

"Now let's go shower and hit the sheets."

In the shower, he fucked her again, and then they were on their way.

"Where are we at?" Zamon asked later when they were in the car. As they rode on through the area, he saw a few spots that reminded him of back home.

"We're on the Northside, Sherwood area. This is where my mama is originally from, before she moved to Tallahassee to go to college."

"That's right. And what did she go to college for again?" he asked curiously, looking out his side window at niggas hanging out on street corners and little children playing in the street.

"She went for social work and got her master's degree, then interned as a counselor for some major organization working with people with mental health issues."

"Like you?" he kidded.

She shoved him playfully. "I'm not crazy, nigga!"

"But you have some mental issues."

"We all do," said Joya. "But it's how you're dealing with those issues that accounts for where you should be in life."

He got quiet all of a sudden.

Joya looked over at him and saw that Zamon had a pensive look on his face, but it was also clear he was worried about something.

"A nickel for your thoughts," she said.

"You do that and I'll be rich." He chuckled, but that still did nothing to sway her curiosity. When she reached to lower the volume of the car's sound system, he knew she was about to pry into his mental vault now.

"There's something on your mind, and I want to know," said Joya. "So tell me, Zee!"

He didn't respond.

"Zamon Khalil Stevenson!" Joya reached over and rubbed his thigh as she drove. "Don't do me like that, bae. I need to know what's on your mind," she said.

"Who is Professor?" he asked.

Instantly, Joya looked over at him, puzzled.

"That's the name you said when we was fuckin' in the shower," he replied. "And not only did you say it one time, but three times. But I guess you was so into me fuckin' you from the back that you didn't realize you'd called me 'Professor'!" Zamon was frowning now.

And now the cat got her tongue.

"Who's quiet now!" he snapped.

"Can I tell you something, bae?" she whispered.

"Don't call me that bullshit! My muthafuckin' name is Zamon. Not bae, and damn sure not no fuckin' Professor!" Zamon was pissed off, and he knew that she was about to give him some bullshit excuse to try and cover her mistake. "And I don't wanna hear no lies!"

"Shut up and listen, please!" she whined.

He snarled at her like he wanted to bite her head off and spit it out the window.

"Yeah, you're right, I do have mental issues. And that's gettin' my pussy fucked every chance I get. I know it's wrong because I have you to do that, but with them it's not special and desiring as it is with you. It's business!"

"You're a trick?" he blurted out.

"Call it what you wanna, but this same trick is the one that keeps your pockets fat and drippin' in nice jewels. Right now I'm a little over a half million dollars strong from what I'm out there doing," said Joya.

"I don't give a fuck about any of that bullshit!" he said with emotion. "I give a fuck about your self-respect and me not having to kill a nigga for disrespectin' you."

That really touched her.

"Matter of fact, stop this fuckin' car. Let me out!"

"Why?" she said.

"Because I can't stand being around your ass right now. Stop the fuckin' car!" he slapped a palm against the dashboard, and its impact startled her. Zamon was heated, and if he stayed in that car with her another minute he was gonna break her jaw.

She stopped the car and let him out.

Big mistake. Wrong territory.

***

Desiree was sitting up in bed when Moya entered the room. She smiled weakly over at her, still a bit tired from being up most of the night. Upon her entry, Moya was frowning, and that wiped the girl's smile off her face.

"What's the matter, Mo?" the girl asked.

"I just bumped into one of the doctors I had a problem with yesterday," Moya replied.

"What problem?" Ella Mae interjected, looking up from her newspaper. Also in the room was little Josh, who peered up at Moya with an interested glance.

Moya glanced down at the boy, confused.

"What the hell is this?" she pointed over at Josh, looking to her grandmother for an explanation.

"I'm Josh!" the boy said, extending his hand.

Moya scowled. "Okay, Josh. You can get the hell out now, Josh," she said.

"Moya!" Ella Mae gave her that testy look Moya knew so well.

"Dez said you were mean," Josh added.

"Oh really?" Moya looked at the girl.

Desiree smiled sweetly up at Moya as Josh said his goodbyes and rolled up out of there.

When he was gone, Moya turned back to her grandmother with a meaningful expression on her face.

"Mama, I know you ain't got no little saltine cracker up in here tryna get with Dez," she said.

"I most certainly do not, child. I found him already in here when I went to grab some fresh blankets."

Moya glanced at Desiree. "You little thot!"

"What's a thot?" asked Ella Mae.

"That hoe over there!" Moya pointed at Desiree, and the old lady came up out of her chair, sending Moya running over to the other side of the room.

Desiree thought that was hilarious.

With a shake of her head, Ella Mae watched as Moya roughed the girl up a little, causing her to explode with laughter. When she saw the first sign of Desiree wincing, she told them to stop horsing around.

Obeying the old lady's command, Moya climbed up onto the bed with Desiree and pulled her into her arms. Then she asked about the phone call Desiree had made to her.

"I met your daddy," said Desiree.

"My daddy?"

"Yep. He's not dead."

Moya looked down at the girl strangely.

"She's not kiddin', Moya," Ella Mae added with the tone of someone dead serious. "My son is very much alive, and Lord knows I'm grateful that he is."

This made Moya get down from the bed, because she knew her grandmother wouldn't bullshit about something like this. Besides, the evidence of truth lay within her weary eyes as Moya looked into them.

How could this be? thought Moya. *Where was he?*

"Your father has left to go tend to some much-needed business, but he'll be back. He had no choice but to come back," said Ella Mae, her eyes misty with emotion.

"I stabbed him too, Mo," said Desiree.

"Twice," Ella Mae added.

"What!" Moya was beyond astounded by this whole thing.

"Let me start from the beginning," said Ella Mae.

"Yeah," said Moya. "You need to do that." She then took a seat in one of the chairs beside the bed near the big window. "Tell me everything," she replied.

And everything she was told, as her grandmother shared with her the moment she opened her eyes and saw Roland up until that very moment.

But Moya didn't like what her loving grandmother was telling her. The man Moya had always known as her father was a standup guy, a boss nigga, one who relied on loyalty and integrity to survive in the streets. Her father had been a man to be feared and respected as the gangster he was. Not the man whom her grandmother was describing to her now. This was a nigga to be looked down upon, a nigga whose death was a certainty where she came from. Because he was nothing but a weak-hearted ass nigga who worked a deal with the Feds to get his time cut.

That was unacceptable in Moya's eyes.

That was flawed as fuck.

"He did it to get back home to us," said Ella Mae once she recognized her granddaughter's disdain.

"No the fuck that nigga didn't, Mama. He did it because he was, and still is, a bitch ass who let them crackaz break his spirit and went against the code."

"Moya, calm down, child."

"That nigga ain't my muthafuckin' daddy, Mama!"

"Moya . . ." Ella Mae rose to her feet, her expression stern. "You better settle down before I do it for you."

That shit went in one ear and out the other.

Moya had no understanding at that point. "I'm tellin' you right now, Mama, if that man comes near me I'ma blow his muthafuckin' face off!"

"You will not do no such thing!"

"Watch me." Moya looked her dead in the eyes and walked out of the room without a backward glance.

***

Detective Shane Rogers had reviewed the surveillance tape from the Circle-E gas station, jotting down all the names that he knew belonged to the faces in the video. He only got four of them he knew by heart, one of them being none other than Jon Boi himself.

The other three were Moya's boys, not to mention the remaining two whose names he didn't know.

If there hadn't been a murder involved, then he wouldn't be looking at the tape. During what appeared to be a hectic situation for Remy before Jon Boi pulled up and interfered, their standing out in the open was good enough reason for someone to do a drive-by.

In the midst of bullets flying, an innocent bystander who was exiting the gas station got shot down. She had been a young Black mother of five, whose kids were still at home waiting on her to get back.

Her death marked the nineteenth casualty, on top of the other four that came after that.

Last night niggas were dropping like flies.

The city was on lockdown now for any muthafucker that looked like they were from the streets. The Feds were in town, and that alone had everybody on pause. The streets now—you could hear a rat piss on cotton.

It was quiet as kept.

But not Rogers, who destroyed the tape for obvious reasons, as he snatched up his jacket and hit the door. He had a bone to pick with Jon Boi, and there was no way he was gonna be quiet about it.

Time to get some straightening for a change.

He needed some closure.

Rogers was down Pensacola Street nearing Orange Avenue, which was located on the southside. He knew that Jon Boi owned an urban clothing store there. That's his baby right there, the detective was aware of how much pride the young hustler took in running that store. It was also said to be a one-stop-shop business.

Jon Boi wasn't no peon.

Rogers pulled up into the entrance of the Ghetto Fresh clothing store and got out. Standing outside the building were two of Jon Boi's homeboys. They didn't even tuck tail and run at the sight of him.

"What's up, Fangz? Mario?" The detective knew them both by names and status; he also knew they were strapped with that heat too.

Fangz, who indeed got his name for having long fangs which he jeweled in platinum, was the first to speak up.

"You comin' to get ghetto fresh, Detective?"

"Ghetto fabulous," he said.

The two homies stepped aside and allowed him to enter the building. Upon his entry, he heard DaBaby's "Vibez" single booming from the surround sound speakers.

"Just the man I need to see," said the detective as he rubbed his palms together. Jon Boi was perched on the main cashier's counter, grinning down at a pretty jet-black petite bitch with bow legs. Even Rogers had to look at that ass and those thighs beneath her Prada dress.

Jon Boi jumped down from the counter and stared across the room at the detective. Then Rogers began browsing around the store like he was interested in buying a Coogi outfit and Gucci loafers.

"What do you want, man?" Jon Boi had strode over next to the detective while he was actually trying on a pair of $1,500 loafers.

"I saw the Circle-E video just now, Jon Boi."

"Okay." He didn't budge.

"And I destroyed the evidence before the wrong person saw it," Rogers replied.

"And you expect me to believe that?"

"Why isn't the whole goddamn task force shuttin' this place down right now after witnessing you conducting a gun battle with a bunch of delinquents? I don't give a damn what you believe or don't believe." Detective Rogers looked up at him from where he sat upon the padded bench with one brown leather Gucci loafer on his foot.

Letting out a frustrated sigh, Jon Boi said, "What do you want, Shane?"

"I wanna retire from all this mess."

Jon Boi cocked his head to the side. "Retire?"

"Yep." Rogers stood up to see how the shoe fit on his foot. "Nice," he said. Then he looked back up at the hustler. "Roland is back," he said.

"Huh?" Jon Boi's eyebrows raised.

"He's back, nephew," said Rogers. "And you damn sure can't let him find out you shot him that night."

And that, Jon Boi thought, was definitely not happening. He had better find Roland before Roland found out the truth.

Chapter 15

Guess who was waiting on Nicholas Vontelli when the Feds released him after hours of interrogating him, trying to get him to cough up information he didn't have? The last person he least expected to see after all these years of pain and suffering.

And the only woman who had once possessed his heart. The only woman who knew the true him.

Nicholas, no longer playing the role of a paralyzed man, stepped out into the bright sunshine before the building's entrance. He was a free man again, but not without now having the Feds watching him closely.

There was a long, shiny black limo waiting for him at the curb, and one of the most beautiful women alive leaning directly against it.

"My god. Linda. Is it really you?" he spoke up, reaching out his hand to her, for his other arm was in a sling.

"It's me," she batted her eyes dazzlingly.

"You're beautiful," he said, wincing from his flesh wound.

"Aren't I always? C'mon, let's get away from this place. It makes me nervous knowing they're watching you, and I may be implicated now in something I have no clue about." With that said, they both got into the limo and drove off, distancing themselves as far away from the place as possible.

Nicholas sat next to Linda, taking in every curve, every wrinkle, everything that made her so magnificently gorgeous. He breathed in her lovely aroma and sighed with contentment. But there was still a throbbing sensation near his heart at having to face her again after all these years.

Fifty years, to be exact.

Fifty years of running away with his twin brother and leaving him to fend for himself.

"Question," Linda replied. "How in the hell did you manage to escape their clutches after all that happened?"

"I was hoping you could answer that question, Linda."

He accepted the wine she offered him.

"They didn't have nothing on me. I showed up after everything had went down." He sipped his drink. "But I wasn't the man they really wanted—they wanted William." Nicholas's injured shoulder was agonizing, but he had enough wine there to soothe his worries. "They knew what he did to me."

"But they shot you, though," she insisted.

"And William has done worse," he said, reminding her of his brother's betrayal, and hers as well.

163

A long silence ensued.

"I was young and weak, Nicholas. I let your brother talk me into running away with him. I didn't know the truth of what he'd done to you until three years later. He made me cut off all contact with everybody, saying the mafia was after us. I was stupid to believe him, Nicholas, you gotta believe me," she pleaded.

"So he said the mafia did that to me?"

"Yes," she said. "He did."

Nicholas laughed.

"Do you forgive me, Nicholas? Even at sixty-eight years old I'm still struggling with my weakness."

"How did you know where to find William when the FBI didn't even know?" he asked.

She looked over at him with surprise.

"Did William contact you somehow?"

"No," she said.

"Then how did you know?"

"Patrick," she said.

"Patrick?"

"My son. I abandoned him when he was two years old. When I found out what William had done to you, I ran away, leaving my son with that monster. I admit I was an unfit mother by doing that, and I regret every second of it to this day."

Her sorrow affected Nicholas in the worst way. He wanted to pull her to him, but his injured arm prevented him from doing that.

He was still weak too, very weak indeed.

"And now my son is dead." Linda put her head in her hands and cried like a baby. "He was shot dead in that house last night."

"I'm sorry," Nicholas whispered to her.

"I know." Linda suddenly came up with the switchblade in her hand and slit Nicholas's throat from ear to ear. In a surprised expression, he stared at her as he reached for his neck. The flow of blood was coming out like a waterfall, draining his life away from him.

"And you know what too, Nicholas?" said Linda as she poured herself another drink.

He looked at her in the last seconds of his life.

"I'm still the queen," she said and downed her drink. "I'll tell you about it when we meet again."

And he was gone.

Dead.

***

They were just leaving *Yours Truly Catering Services*, which was Naomi's prized business establishment, headed for Toya's favorite place to visit whenever she was in the city. And that was Cookie's Bakery downtown, a business that Naomi helped her aunt get off the ground.

The woman went from baking biscuits and pies and serving them to the block hustlers, to running her very own bakery serving the whole city.

Auntie Cookie was Toya's road dawg, and she would definitely be happy to see her.

The bakery wasn't that far from *Yours Truly Catering*, so they made it there in less than ten minutes. And when they entered the building, mouth-watering aromas from every variety of bakery products teased their cravings.

Cookie was in the middle of fussing with one of her workers behind the counter when, out the corner of her eye, she glimpsed her sister. Then, once she laid eyes on Toya, the big woman shrieked with joy.

And the whole damn building shook as she came running into Toya's open arms.

"Hey, Auntie!" Toya kissed her on the cheek. It had been almost a year since they saw one another.

"It's about damn time you came to visit ole' Cookie. Where are the other two? I saw Moya recently, but that fast one, Joya—she's a slippery little rascal."

"She's here too."

"Where? I don't see her," said Cookie.

Naomi gave her sister a hard look. "I'm pretty sure she'll get around to it," she said. Then she disappeared somewhere behind the counter through a side door.

"What's her problem?" Cookie replied.

"It's a long story, Auntie," Toya sighed miserably. "But I do miss you, though. Where is Daisy?"

"In the back labeling deliveries." Cookie resembled the actress Tisha Campbell, but to a much heavier effect. "You know I'm doing house calls, delivery now?"

"That means your shit is booming!"

"Booming real good!" Cookie let out a big laugh.

Toya wanted to see her cousin Daisy, who was Cookie's twenty-four-year-old daughter. Daisy had been her truest friend growing up in Jacksonville, and even one of her major influences in becoming a school teacher. So when Cookie said she knew just what to get to welcome her back—which she was referring to as Toya's favorite banana pound cake with caramel glaze—she told her to tell Daisy she was there too.

That banana-stuffed pound cake was the bomb. Toya couldn't wait to get her shot at it again.

Like lightning fast, Cookie brought her two thick slices on a platter, added a cold cup of lemonade, and handed her a fork to dig in with.

"Dang, that was fast," said Toya.

"That's why my business is good—because I don't keep the customers waitin' long. Now, let's go have a seat so you can tell me all about what's going on. Your mama ain't gonna tell me everything like you will."

"What makes you think that?"

Cookie hooked an arm around hers. "Because I'm your favorite auntie, that's why."

"I don't do favoritism," said Toya.

"You will today!"

They found a seat near the front of the bakery, which overlooked the main highway. The place was once a family-owned barbecue joint until things went sour, and Naomi leased the building from under the competition's scrutiny. That was four years ago, and look at it now.

As Toya explained to her aunt what was going on back in Tallahassee, she herself was becoming agitated. She was wondering how her twin was doing, and Desiree, and Ella Mae; she was worried about all her loved ones she left behind just to appease her mother.

Toya felt like crying, really, because she did exactly what she vowed to never do.

And that's neglect her students the way she did.

"That's some messed up shit right there."

"Tell me about it!" Toya said moments before her phone came to life. When she recognized Joya's number, she told Cookie and answered the phone.

"Tell her I said get her narrow tail here right now," said Cookie.

Toya held up a patient finger as she listened to what sounded like her sister crying. "Joya? What's wrong?" she said, her heart warming up with panic.

"He don't want me no more," Joya cried.

"What? Who? Where is Zamon, Joya?"

"Zamon gone!" she said.

"Gone where?"

"I don't know. He just got out the car and ran away." She cried some more, sounding pathetic as hell.

"Where are you right now, Joya?" Toya asked, and she told her. "Stay right there, twin. I'm on my way!" she said as she shot up to her feet. Toya promised her again that she was on her way and asked Cookie to go get her mother.

"Daisy's on her way out now," said Cookie.

"Perfect," she replied.

Little did she know it would already be too late.

***

Zamon wasn't trying to hear none of that shit Joya was talking. That's why he jumped out the car and ran from her ass, making sure that she didn't follow him. But of course she did anyway, so he had to manipulate the situation.

Just when she thought he had gone into a local shopping center to distract himself with something to do, he slipped out the back emergency door on her ass. Yes, he was being overly dramatic about the situation, but he really wasn't thinking rationally—Joya had his head all fucked up. Now here he was, trekking down the sidewalk on unknown territory and wearing his emotions on his sleeve.

Zamon should know better than that.

Where was his street smarts? Where was that same street nigga who respected the game for what it was?

Zamon reached inside his pocket for some smokes and came up empty. He remembered smoking his last cigarette last night. Good thing there was a convenience store up ahead because he really needed to get his lungs out the pond.

He entered the store and found an older Black guy behind the counter. He strode down the side aisle toward the beverages section and chose a bottle of orange Fanta soda to drink. Next, he made his way back to the counter just as two ghetto booty Black chicks walked in. He nodded at them in passing and caught the whiff of weed smoke wafting off their bodies.

One of the females approached the counter while the other one with the microbraids went the other way. Now Zamon had to stand behind all this ass lil' mama was packing in them jeans. Zamon looked down at himself and noted that he was still looking fresh in his Fendi outfit and smoke gray and black Air Maxes.

Shit, he was still looking good in the same shit he had on yesterday.

"Gimme a box of peach White Owls and a pack of cigarillos," said the girl who looked a lot like Dej Loaf.

Zamon couldn't help but notice her thick wad of cash.

"You burnin' good, ain't you?" he said.

"Something like that," she smirked over her shoulder at him, briefly taking in his jewels and gear. "Who are you? I never seen you before," she said.

"I'm Zamon," he said. "And you?"

"Dominique."

"And I'm Shannon," came the voice of the other female coming up behind Zamon. She had all types of goodies in her hands; them bitches had the munchies.

"What's up?" Zamon said, pulling out his own thick stack of bills and peeling off a twenty, handing it to the store clerk. "Add a pack of Newports to all that, sir," he said. "Regular, shorts."

"I pay for my own stuff," said Dominique.

"Not today you're not. I'm just visitin' from out of town, so consider it my treat."

"Out of town where?" said Shannon.

He told them, and both females smiled at each other, and Dominique made sure to back all that ass up against his dick on the sly.

Zamon followed them outside and asked Dominique what was up with him buying some weed.

"My brotha got that gas," said Dominique.

"That pressure!" Shannon added.

He nodded. "I wouldn't spend my money on anything but that pressure," said Zamon.

"Well, we gotta go back to the house to get it."

"I'm down with that." Zamon wasn't even thinking as he got into the car with these two bitches he didn't even know. It wasn't until they pulled up outside the house that he realized his mistake. There were about six niggas on the porch and in the front yard.

"Come on, Zamon!" said Shannon.

Zamon touched the gun tucked beneath his shirt just to make sure it was there.

"You gettin' out or what?" Dominique asked.

With an unsettling breath, Zamon got out of the car, and then all eyes were on him. But one thing he knew he shouldn't do was let them see him sweat. Any sign of intimidation would be bad for him, so Zamon lifted his head high and let Dominique lead the way to her big brother.

The worst decision she could have ever made.

Zamon was a stranger.

A nobody to them.

And now he wished he had never jumped out the car with Joya.

Because shit was about to get real.

Chapter 16

The room was quiet as Roland dropped his head in his hands and willed his racing heart to calm down. But how could it, when it was just held in a vicious chokehold by the words Doughboy had just spoken? The reality of his view of the situation was so surreal that Roland couldn't help but be reminded of his old self.

Had his daughter become him now?

When he spoke to his mother earlier, she had beat around the bush with him where Moya was concerned. But Doughboy had just given it to him raw and uncut.

Moya was a gangster.

Nothing less.

Now Roland wondered how Naomi had put up with this all these years. To hear how Toya was chasing her dreams of becoming a great school teacher made his heart sigh with contentment. Then Joya's passion for helping others and braving the music school thing was pleasing to him as well. Regardless of the fact that she was said to have grown a welcoming sexual appetite, Roland figured he could get around that and help her refocus on what mattered most.

He had to give it to Naomi—she had done well with the girls, despite their imperfections.

But this deal with Moya had him blown; he really wanted to know her story—to know the moment she decided to be a gangster and not the pro basketball player she once dreamed of being. And that's when he remembered her being shot in the hand that night, too.

"Damn," he whispered softly. So instead of shooting baskets now, his daughter was out there shooting pistols. Doughboy had already told him of three murders she was said to have committed, but no evidence had been brought forward, which worked out in her favor.

"Are you gonna tell her the truth?" said Doughboy, seeing how the whole situation was affecting his cousin.

Roland raised his head and met Doughboy's gaze.

"Because I'm tellin' you now, cuz, that girl isn't gonna respect what you did. Maybe the other two would understand, but Moya? Imagine saying some shit like that to the old Roland who taught me the game," said Doughboy.

"I can't lie to her, cuz."

"Hey," Doughboy threw his hands up. "I'm just saying, cuz—Moya is not the one to be underestimated."

"I'll take your word for it."

"You better."

Was his cousin telling him that he should be afraid of his own daughter?

"I need to borrow your whip for a little while, cuz. I need to get around lowkey for a few days."

Doughboy tossed him the car keys.

"Hold my shit down as much as you want. Shit, I got four more at the crib."

"You're doing it big like that?" Roland teased.

Doughboy saluted him. "You taught me well," he said.

Fifteen minutes later, Roland was rolling back towards Tallahassee in a shiny black Mercedes-Benz coupe. So much for getting around lowkey, but it was better than an Uber cab. Never in his life did he want to ever ride in one of those again. The muthafucker smelled like toe jams and cheap perfume.

His next destination was to visit his old side bitch, Lisa, who still lived over there off Jackson Bluff. He heard she hadn't come to his "doctored-up" funeral ceremony. But he figured he already knew why—it would have probably turned out badly if Naomi saw her.

Naomi and Lisa didn't see eye to eye.

Naomi had whipped her ass once. So it was best that he dealt with her ass in her own space.

It was a Saturday, so he hoped to find Lisa home chillin' with her feet kicked up. He heard she was working over at the local Super Walmart and doing good for herself too. He was actually proud of her, because Lisa wasn't the 9-to-5 type of chick when he last saw her.

Lisa Sherman was always the hustler, the diva.

She had game.

Time changes people for better or for worse, and Roland guessed she assumed the simple life was better.

When he pulled up at her address, he saw an old white Chrysler 300 parked in her driveway. Roland parked at the curb and got out of the car. Then he fished out his cellphone and dialed her number.

She answered on the second ring. "Hello?"

"It's Roland. If you don't believe it's me, all you gotta do is come outside," he said. When he didn't get a response, he took it as though she was still processing the shock of recognizing his voice. Then he saw the window curtains move, heard a surprised gasp over the phone, and then the front door opened.

Damn was all Roland could say when he finally laid eyes on her. Ten years had done her well. Lisa was looking damn good. She looked thicker and sexier than ever now.

And then she ran towards him.

"Is it really you, Roland?" she said after coming to a halt two feet before him.

"I'm not dead," he smirked.

Then she threw her arms around him.

But that happiness was short-lived when Roland inquired about his estranged son.

Lisa sighed. "I haven't seen Tron in two days."

"What's up with him?"

"Out there running the streets with his crew."

"And who is his crew?" Roland asked.

Again, Lisa sighed deeply. "Your daughter and her youngins," she replied, and that's when he feared the worst.

Meanwhile, Moya was hanging out with some of her youngins in the trap house. She had them shut up shop since the Feds were in town. And since they were snatching muthafuckers up left and right out there, Moya decided to lay low for a bit. She didn't want to risk herself or any of her youngins being apprehended by the police. So for now it was just chill mode and relax a little; she'd had a busy week.

She had to respect the forces that be.

Live to see another day.

But what she didn't respect was this latest revelation of her father's resurrection. The nigga might think this shit is sweet, but he got another thing coming. And just to be true to her youngins, she told them all about it, and they clowned on that nigga. And while they clowned him, Moya tried to visualize just what he might look like today.

Then her dislike for the nigga cut that short. She couldn't even think about him without frowning.

Roland played.

And the nigga is still playing.

One thing she won't do if he ever shows his face around her is play. Moya had no love, no respect for niggas like him. He burned that bridge the moment he decided to go against the street code. Her father, who was once seen as one of the most respected and feared men in the game, faked his death in order to take down his drug connect while working with the FBI.

She couldn't wait to blow his brains out.

A call came in and she checked the display to see who it was.

"What it do, Dee?" she answered. She was referring to Devon Palmer, a major dope boy from the Joe Louis projects, Bang's homeboy. Her and Devon were good; they had mad respect for one another.

"Everything's kosher on this side," he said. "But I just got word them boys on your side of town right now!"

Moya snapped her fingers and everybody in the room looked up. "Y'all clean this bitch up!" she said. "The Feds close by," she said before turning her attention back to Devon. "Bet that up, Dee. I owe you one," Moya told him.

"You don't owe me shit!" he retorted. "It's what I do!"

"I love your red ass anyway, nigga!"

"Love," Devon said and hung up.

There were six shooters in the house, and four of them got up to situate things and double-check the spot. There was not to be no guns or dope in the house at that point. All except for her gun, of course—she had no desire to go unarmed for any reason.

Unless Ella Mae said so.

And she's yet to get her pistol back!

After one of her youngins tossed aside the Xbox 360 controller to go check on things, she slid into his spot and took possession of the controller. Lil' Petey and Tyree's closest crony, Animal, were playing the new Mortal Kombat game, and from the looks of it, Animal was getting his ass beat.

"C'mon, Lil Petey, and get some of this shit."

"You don't know nothin', Mo!" he grabbed the other controller back. "Let's start over fresh."

"Nah, fuck that. I wanna help Animal's man get back on some gangsta shit."

"Okay." He accepted the challenge.

Before long, all six of her youngins were raising the roof as Moya and Lil Petey battled back and forth. Outside, Ray Ray and Bizkit peeped in on them from their post, wondering what in the hell was going on.

Out the corner of her eye, Moya saw Tron reach for his ringing phone and escape into the kitchen.

"Nigga, Scorpion is the truth!" she said when she spanked his ass the second time in a row.

A minute later, Tron beckoned her into the kitchen and she went to see what he wanted. Upon entering, Moya saw that he was worried about something—he was sporting one of those long faces.

"I need to go home," he said.

She just looked at him, patiently waiting for him to continue talking.

"Mama is worried sick about me, Moya. She hasn't seen me in two days," he added.

"Family comes first, Tron," said Moya.

He nodded.

"But you don't have to ask my permission for some shit like that. You a man now, boo; all I ask of you is to be safe," she said.

"But I don't wanna leave y'all."

"You got no other choice, Tron," said Moya. "When Mama calls, you better come running every time." And she meant that literally—every time her mama called, she was coming full speed ahead.

***

She had found her brother, PeeWee, out on the back porch having a heated conversation with someone on the house phone. Dominique gave her brother that look that meant she needed him to hurry up. PeeWee gave her a patient finger, and she folded her arms stubbornly.

PeeWee was a fat muthafucker but with swag, having used his hustle game to keep up in the latest fashion and the best of jewels. All from selling weed and running one of the biggest gambling houses on the eastside. The nigga was on his shit for real—PeeWee was about his issue.

"What's up, sis?" PeeWee hung up a minute later.

"I got some big money for you inside."

"Oh yeah?" His brown eyes twinkled.

Dominique then led him back through the back door, up the hallway towards the front of the house.

In the living room, there stood Shannon and Zamon, talking amongst themselves as Shannon proceeded to roll a cigarillo blunt. When PeeWee entered the room, both of them turned their gazes on him. Ignoring Shannon and her phony ass, PeeWee regarded Zamon with silent attentiveness, sizing him up as he tried to see if he knew him or not.

"What's up, nigga?"

"Bruh, this is Zamon," said Dominique. "He's from out of town visitin' his people—"

"Hold up, hold up, hold up!" PeeWee was shaking his head. "Are you tellin' me you don't know this fool?"

"I just met him up at the store."

"And you brought this muthafucker in my house? Bitch, this nigga could be the goddamn Feds!" he bellowed.

She didn't respond to that but cast a worried glance over at Zamon. Zamon shook his head warily.

"Nigga, get the fuck out my house!" PeeWee glared at Zamon.

"PeeWee—" Dominique started, but was then backhanded in the mouth, and she hit the floor.

"Aye, JoJo, Dre, Twin!" PeeWee called out.

Suddenly the front door opened, and two niggas burst inside the house, just as Zamon upped his pistol and dropped the first nigga with a slug to the face. Out of fear and desperate instinct, Zamon sent three more rounds into the second nigga. He flew back through the front door as each bullet punched him in the chest.

Dominique screamed and ducked for cover.

Shannon was shocked still.

And PeeWee, whom Zamon caught out the corner of his eye reaching for something beneath the sofa cushion, caught one to the middle of his wide back.

Another one of PeeWee's homeboys peeped his head in the door, and Zamon sent two bullets his way.

Then he took off running down the nearby hallway from which Dominique and her brother had come a minute ago. When he noticed the back door, he snatched it open and got missing. To his surprise, there was a wooded area behind the house, but there was a small problem, though.

A big beast of a red-nose pitbull was prowling around on a long chain that seemed quite breakable. The dog was massive, almost as big as PeeWee was.

But he was the one with the power, though. Zamon ran for the woods behind the house, and the pitbull waited on him to get closer. Without remorse, Zamon put a bullet through its chest and ran right past the dog.

Shots fired behind him as bullets zoomed past him, hitting trees and branches up ahead.

That was all the encouragement Zamon needed to make him run harder. All he had to do was make it into the woods, and it was all game after that.

He couldn't believe how his stupid decision had almost got him killed. Now he was trapped in a hood he knew nothing about, wishing he had never come to Jacksonville.

Chapter 17

After assuring her mother she could handle the situation herself, Toya took off to go rescue her emotional twin sister. Why she and Zamon were going through it, she had no clue, but she just hoped he didn't put his hands on her. Because if he did, Toya was going to break those same hands and make Joya whip his ass.

But Toya had a feeling about what might have triggered the differences between Zamon and her twin.

Earlier, Naomi had confided in her daughter about the conversation she'd had with Zamon the night before, basically telling him what Toya herself had preached to Joya time and time again. She knew that they both really loved each other; they just went about expressing it in the wrong way.

Joya always wanted things to go her way, and to Joya, she was never wrong.

She had a problem admitting her faults.

"How much you wanna bet that they'll be right back together again before the day is out?" said Daisy.

"I don't doubt that for one second," said Toya. Joya and Zamon always fought, but never really in a physical way. Although this one seemed serious, because her twin had never called her crying her heart out. Joya wasn't the crying type. What have you done, Zamon? thought Toya.

"Guess who's back home now for good," Daisy replied, receiving a curious glance from her cousin.

"I don't do guessing games."

"Not even with your students?" she asked.

"Of course I do; their guessing games aren't complicated. Now tell me who, girl!" Toya said.

"Haaji Miller," said Daisy.

Toya paused and shot her cousin a look.

Haaji was Toya's childhood sweetheart before he broke up with her their senior year in high school. After graduation, he went off to the Navy and was said to have been studying computer technology in the process. Last she heard of Haaji was a year ago, through his baby brother Todd, who said that Haaji was engaged.

When it shouldn't have mattered to her, it truly did, because Haaji had chosen to marry Apryl Lynn, the same girl Toya used to share her seat on the bus with.

"What's up with him?" said Toya.

"He's not married to that girl, if that's what you're thinking. Haaji is back home, running a junior league basketball team and working with juveniles at a second-chance program. He is doing fine, cuz, and looking good too." Daisy smirked and cracked her window to let some air into the car. She too was engaged to her boyfriend of three years, whom Toya liked and thought was good for her cousin.

"That's nice to know," said Toya.

"And he's asked about you too."

"That's nice to know, too," sighed Toya, spinning the bracelet on her wrist that Elijah had given to her as a gift.

And of course, Daisy knew it was best to let the subject die.

No need for creating a bad vibe.

Fuck Haaji Miller.

Soon afterward, they were turning into the entrance of this new pet store off Main Street that Toya didn't recall being there the last time she visited. They spotted Joya's blue Dodge Caliber. Toya got out and moved toward the car at once.

It was empty.

Automatically, Toya's eyes shifted toward the pet store, and she headed in that direction.

As the bell jingled above the entrance door, Toya was hit with a full blast of animal body odor. Joya was in the process of leaving just as her twin stepped through the door.

"C'mon," said Toya, throwing an arm over her shoulders. "Lemme take you to Mama; she's worried about you too."

On their way to the car, Daisy tooted the horn and said she'd stop by the house later.

In the car, Toya angled their journey back in the direction of the bakery. For a moment, the car was quiet except for the constant sighing coming from Joya's side. Toya looked over and saw her twin leaning her head against the window, looking all sad and shit.

"Did he put his hands on you?"

"No," murmured Joya. "Zamon would never hit me."

"Never say never."

"Never," Joya stated firmly.

"Then what happened?" Toya wanted to know. The last time she saw Joya like this was when Zamon went to jail for fighting in the bar over her.

"You don't really wanna know, twin."

"I want the truth, Joya."

And the whole truth she gave her, shocking the hell out of Toya at the same time. It was no wonder Zamon ran from her ass—Joya had freaked him the fuck out.

"A half million dollars, Joya?" Toya gasped.

"More than half," Joya corrected.

"So you're a hooker now?"

"No!" Joya shot her a mean look. "Hell no!"

"Then w-what are you?" asked Toya.

Before Joya could reply, she saw the car veering off into oncoming traffic. When she looked back over at her twin, she saw Toya with her eyes rolled to the back of her head.

Toya was having a seizure behind the wheel.

And they were about to crash.

***

The Benz parked in front of his house caused Tron to wonder who it belonged to. He only knew a few people who owned a Benz, and none of them had business having it parked outside his house.

Owning a Benz of his own was one of his top goals—next to getting his mother out the hood. Moya paid him well— shit, everybody in his crew was playing with twenty stacks or better. She wasn't stingy with her money; Moya wanted to see all of them wealthy.

His measly sixty-two thousand saved up was all blood, sweat, and tears.

At eighteen years old, Tron was making more money than most niggas who'd been hustling damn near twenty years. So at this rate, he'd have his mother living large in no time.

Tron didn't give a fuck how he did it, just as long as she was out the hood.

He got out of the car after parking it behind the Benz. His old-school Bonneville was a far stretch from a Benz, but his shit was sitting clean, though. It didn't have no problem sending pussy his way.

Tron entered the house and found his mother sitting in the living room with some nigga. Whoever he was, Tron felt very uncomfortable with his staring. Then he turned to his mother for an explanation.

"Keltron." His mother stood up. "I have something to tell you, baby," she said.

"That this man is supposed to be my old man?" Tron replied with a look of indifference. "It ain't hard to tell; it's obvious we got the same features."

Lisa glanced at Roland.

"Where you been? In prison? Africa? Some-muthafuckin'-where? Because you obviously didn't give a damn about me or my mama, or else you would've been here from the beginning."

"Tron!" Lisa replied frantically.

"I was here from the beginning," Roland said as he stood up to confront him.

"You wasn't shit, nigga!" Tron snapped.

Roland stepped closer.

"You better back the fuck up," Tron warned him as he reached to his waist for a pistol that wasn't there. Then something in his mind's eye registered—a memory so deep in the back of his mind that it took a minute to surface.

Three feet away, Roland saw the slow process of recollection in Tron's eyes. Then Tron began to back up a couple of feet out of instinct.

"I remember you now," he said.

"The softball game when you were eight years old—I was the one who gave you your first glove. It was your favorite color, red. Or what about when your mother and I took you to Fun Station for your seventh birthday? You don't remember that neither?" said Roland.

He did remember, Tron thought. Although that was many years ago, he still remembered. How could he not remember some of the special moments of his life?

"But what's all that supposed to do for you? You're too late to try and come play daddy now."

"But I'm still here, Tron," he said.

"Nigga, I don't even remember your fuckin' name," Tron replied, looking him in the eyes.

"Roland," he said.

"Roland?"

Roland nodded.

Wasn't Moya's father named Roland? Tron thought. He was certain of it; he then recalled the things Moya had said about her father earlier. As realization struck, it hit Tron in the chest so hard it made him backpedal.

"Tron, what's wrong?" his mother asked him.

Tron stared at the man before him, not believing what his heart was telling him.

Without a word, Tron retrieved his phone and snapped a picture of Roland, then he sent the picture to Moya's phone with a short message.

"Is this your father?" the text read.

"What are you doing, Keltron?" demanded Lisa.

"It's okay, Lisa." Roland knew exactly what Tron was doing, and he let him do it.

It wasn't even a minute later when Moya responded with a call. Tron was almost weary to answer.

"What's up, Mo?" he answered.

"Yeah, that's his bitch ass! How did you get that picture, Tron?" asked Moya.

"I just took the picture myself."

"Where are you, Tron?" Her tone sounded suspicious.

"At my house," he said.

"He's at your fuckin' house?" she gasped.

Tron sighed. "Yeah."

"Then shoot that muthafucka, boo!"

"I can't."

"Why?"

"Because I don't have my strap," he said.

A brief silence ensued.

"Then we coming over," she said and hung up the phone. And that's when Tron knew the ultimate truth.

Moya was his sister.

To Be Continued…

PART 2
WHEN IT RAINS IT POURS:
BY ANY MEANS NECESSARY

Lock Down Publications and Ca$h Presents
Assisted Publishing Packages

Due to an increase in the price of services we have increased our prices. The prices below reflect the price increase as of 11/1/24.

BASIC PACKAGE $699	UPGRADED PACKAGE $1000
Editing Cover Design Formatting	Typing Editing Cover Design Formatting Upload eBooks to Amazon Upload Paperback to Amazon
ADVANCE PACKAGE $1,400	**LDP SUPREME PACKAGE $1,700**
Typing Editing (line editing/content) Cover Design Formatting Copyright Registration Proofreading Upload eBooks to Amazon Upload Paperback to Amazon	Typing Editing (line editing/content) Cover Design Formatting Copyright Registration Proofreading Set up Amazon Account Upload eBooks to Amazon Upload Paperback to Amazon Advertise on LDP's Amazon and Facebook Page

***Other services available upon request.
Additional charges may apply

Lock Down Publications
P.O. Box 944
Stockbridge, GA 30281-9998
Phone: 470 303-9761
Email: lockdownpublications@gmail.com

Submission Guideline

Submit the first three chapters of your completed manuscript to ldpsubmissions@gmail.com. In the subject line add **Your Book's Title**. The manuscript must be in a Word Doc file and sent as an attachment. Document should be in Times New Roman, double spaced, and in size 12 font. Also, provide your synopsis and full contact information. If sending multiple submissions, they must each be in a separate email.

Have a story but no way to send it electronically? You can still submit to LDP/Ca$h Presents. Send in the first three chapters, written or typed, of your completed manuscript to:

LDP: Submissions Dept
P.O. Box 944
Stockbridge, GA 30281-9998

DO NOT send original manuscript. Must be a duplicate.
Provide your synopsis and a cover letter containing your full contact information.

Thanks for considering LDP and Ca$h Presents.

NEW RELEASES

BLOODLINE OF A SAVAGE 1&2
THESE VICIOUS STREETS 1&2
RELENTLESS GOON
RELENTLESS GOON 2
BY PRINCE A. TAUHID

THE BUTTERFLY MAFIA 1-3
BY FUMIYA PAYNE

A THUG'S STREET PRINCESS 1&2
BY MEESHA

CITY OF SMOKE 2
BY MOLOTTI

STEPPERS 1,2&3
THE REAL BADDIES OF CHI-RAQ
BY KING RIO

THE LANE 1&2
BY KEN-KEN SPENCE

THUG OF SPADES 1&2
LOVE IN THE TRENCHES 2
CORNER BOYS
BY COREY ROBINSON

TIL DEATH 3
BY ARYANNA

THE BIRTH OF A GANGSTER 4
BY DELMONT PLAYER

PRODUCT OF THE STREETS 1&2
BY DEMOND "MONEY" ANDERSON

NO TIME FOR ERROR
BY KEESE

MONEY HUNGRY DEMONS
BY TRANAY ADAMS

Coming Soon from Lock Down Publications/Ca$h Presents

IF YOU CROSS ME ONCE 6
ANGEL V
By Anthony Fields

IMMA DIE BOUT MINE 5
By Aryanna

A THUGS STREET PRINCESS 3
By Meesha

PRODUCT OF THE STREETS 3
By Demond Money Anderson

CORNER BOYS 2
By Corey Robinson

THE MURDER QUEENS 6&7
By Michael Gallon

CITY OF SMOKE 3
By Molotti

CONFESSIONS OF A DOPE BOY
By Nicholas Lock

THA TAKEOVER
By Keith Chandler

BETRAYAL OF A G 2
By Ray Vinci

CRIME BOSS
By Playa Ray

Available Now

RESTRAINING ORDER 1 & 2
By **CA$H & Coffee**

LOVE KNOWS NO BOUNDARIES 1-3
By **Coffee**

RAISED AS A GOON I, II, III & IV
BRED BY THE SLUMS I, II, III
BLAST FOR ME I & II
ROTTEN TO THE CORE I II III
A BRONX TALE I, II, III
DUFFLE BAG CARTEL I II III IV V VI
HEARTLESS GOON I II III IV V
A SAVAGE DOPEBOY I II
DRUG LORDS I II III
CUTTHROAT MAFIA I II
KING OF THE TRENCHES
By **Ghost**

LAY IT DOWN I & II
LAST OF A DYING BREED I II
BLOOD STAINS OF A SHOTTA I & II III
By **Jamaica**

LOYAL TO THE GAME I II III
LIFE OF SIN I, II III
By **TJ & Jelissa**

IF LOVING HIM IS WRONG…I & II
LOVE ME EVEN WHEN IT HURTS I II III
By **Jelissa**

PUSH IT TO THE LIMIT
By **Bre' Hayes**

BLOODY COMMAS I & II
SKI MASK CARTEL I, II & III
KING OF NEW YORK I II, III IV V
RISE TO POWER I II III
COKE KINGS I II III IV V
BORN HEARTLESS I II III IV
KING OF THE TRAP I II
By **T.J. Edwards**

WHEN THE STREETS CLAP BACK I & II III
THE HEART OF A SAVAGE I II III IV
MONEY MAFIA I II
LOYAL TO THE SOIL I II III
By **Jibril Williams**

A DISTINGUISHED THUG STOLE MY HEART I II & III
LOVE SHOULDN'T HURT I II III IV
RENEGADE BOYS 1-4
PAID IN KARMA 1-3
SAVAGE STORMS 1-3
AN UNFORESEEN LOVE 1-3
BABY, I'M WINTERTIME COLD 1-3
A THUG'S STREET PRINCESS 1&2
By **Meesha**

A GANGSTER'S CODE 1-3
A GANGSTER'S SYN 1-3
THE SAVAGE LIFE 1-3
CHAINED TO THE STREETS 1-3
BLOOD ON THE MONEY 1-3
A GANGSTA'S PAIN 1-3
BEAUTIFUL LIES AND UGLY TRUTHS
CHURCH IN THESE STREETS
By **J-Blunt**

CUM FOR ME 1-8
An LDP Erotica Collaboration

BLOOD OF A BOSS 1-5
SHADOWS OF THE GAME
TRAP BASTARD
By **Askari**

THE STREETS BLEED MURDER 1-3
THE HEART OF A GANGSTA 1-3
By **Jerry Jackson**

WHEN A GOOD GIRL GOES BAD
By **Adrienne**

THE COST OF LOYALTY 1-3
By **Kweli**

BRIDE OF A HUSTLA 1-3
THE FETTI GIRLS 1-3
CORRUPTED BY A GANGSTA 1-4
BLINDED BY HIS LOVE
THE PRICE YOU PAY FOR LOVE 1-3
DOPE GIRL MAGIC 1-3
By **Destiny Skai**

A KINGPIN'S AMBITION
A KINGPIN'S AMBITION II
I MURDER FOR THE DOUGH
By **Ambitious**

TRUE SAVAGE 1-7
DOPE BOY MAGIC 1-3
MIDNIGHT CARTEL 1-3
CITY OF KINGZ 1&2
NIGHTMARE ON SILENT AVE
THE PLUG OF LIL MEXICO 1&2
CLASSIC CITY
By **Chris Green**

A GANGSTER'S REVENGE 1-4
THE BOSS MAN'S DAUGHTERS 1-5
A SAVAGE LOVE 1&2
BAE BELONGS TO ME 1&2
A HUSTLER'S DECEIT 1-3
WHAT BAD BITCHES DO 1-3
SOUL OF A MONSTER 1-3
KILL ZONE
A DOPE BOY'S QUEEN 1-3
TIL DEATH 1-3
IMMA DIE BOUT MINE 1-4
By **Aryanna**

A DOPEBOY'S PRAYER
By **Eddie "Wolf" Lee**

THE KING CARTEL 1-3
By **Frank Gresham**

THESE NIGGAS AIN'T LOYAL 1-3
By **Nikki Tee**

GANGSTA SHYT 1-3
By **CATO**

THE ULTIMATE BETRAYAL
By **Phoenix**

BOSS'N UP 1-3
By **Royal Nicole**

I LOVE YOU TO DEATH
By **Destiny J**

I RIDE FOR MY HITTA
I STILL RIDE FOR MY HITTA
By **Misty Holt**

LOVE & CHASIN' PAPER
By **Qay Crockett**

TO DIE IN VAIN
SINS OF A HUSTLA
By **ASAD**

BROOKLYN HUSTLAZ
By **Boogsy Morina**

BROOKLYN ON LOCK 1 & 2
By **Sonovia**

GANGSTA CITY
By **Teddy Duke**

A DRUG KING AND HIS DIAMOND 1-3
A DOPEMAN'S RICHES
HER MAN, MINE'S TOO 1&2
CASH MONEY HO'S
THE WIFEY I USED TO BE 1&2
PRETTY GIRLS DO NASTY THINGS
By **Nicole Goosby**

LIPSTICK KILLAH 1-3
CRIME OF PASSION 1-3
FRIEND OR FOE 1-3
By **Mimi**

TRAPHOUSE KING 1-3
KINGPIN KILLAZ 1-3
STREET KINGS 1&2
PAID IN BLOOD 1&2
CARTEL KILLAZ 1-3
DOPE GODS 1&2
By **Hood Rich**

THE STREETS ARE CALLING
By **Duquie Wilson**

STEADY MOBBN' 1-3
THE STREETS STAINED MY SOUL 1-3
By **Marcellus Allen**

WHO SHOT YA 1-3
SON OF A DOPE FIEND 1-4
HEAVEN GOT A GHETTO 1&2
SKI MASK MONEY 1&2
By **Renta**

GORILLAZ IN THE BAY 1-4
TEARS OF A GANGSTA 1/&2
3X KRAZY 1&2
STRAIGHT BEAST MODE 1&2
By **DE'KARI**

TRIGGADALE 1-3
MURDA WAS THE CASE 1-3
By **Elijah R. Freeman**

SLAUGHTER GANG 1-3
RUTHLESS HEART 1-3
By **Willie Slaughter**

GOD BLESS THE TRAPPERS 1-3
THESE SCANDALOUS STREETS 1-3
FEAR MY GANGSTA 1-5
THESE STREETS DON'T LOVE NOBODY 1-2
BURY ME A G 1-5
A GANGSTA'S EMPIRE 1-4
THE DOPEMAN'S BODYGAURD 1&2
THE REALEST KILLAZ 1-3
THE LAST OF THE OGS 1-3
By **Tranay Adams**

MARRIED TO A BOSS 1-3
By **Destiny Skai & Chris Green**

KINGZ OF THE GAME 1-7
CRIME BOSS 1-3
By **Playa Ray**

FUK SHYT
By **Blakk Diamond**

DON'T F#CK WITH MY HEART 1&2
By **Linnea**

ADDICTED TO THE DRAMA 1-3
IN THE ARM OF HIS BOSS
By **Jamila**

LOYALTY AIN'T PROMISED 1&2
By **Keith Williams**

YAYO 1-4
A SHOOTER'S AMBITION 1&2
BRED IN THE GAME
By **S. Allen**

TRAP GOD 1-3
RICH $AVAGE 1-3
MONEY IN THE GRAVE 1-3
CARTEL MONEY
By **Martell Troublesome Bolden**

FOREVER GANGSTA 1&2
GLOCKS ON SATIN SHEETS 1&2
By **Adrian Dulan**

TOE TAGZ 1-4
LEVELS TO THIS SHYT 1&2
IT'S JUST ME AND YOU
By **Ah'Million**

KILLAZ ON STANDBY | IRA B.

KINGPIN DREAMS 1-3
RAN OFF ON DA PLUG
By **Paper Boi Rari**

THE STREETS MADE ME 1-3
By **Larry D. Wright**

CONFESSIONS OF A GANGSTA 1-4
CONFESSIONS OF A JACKBOY 1-3
CONFESSIONS OF A HITMAN
By **Nicholas Lock**

I'M NOTHING WITHOUT HIS LOVE
SINS OF A THUG
TO THE THUG I LOVED BEFORE
A GANGSTA SAVED XMAS
IN A HUSTLER I TRUST
By **Monet Dragun**

QUIET MONEY 1-3
THUG LIFE 1-3
EXTENDED CLIP 1&2
A GANGSTA'S PARADISE
By **Trai'Quan**

CAUGHT UP IN THE LIFE 1-3
THE STREETS NEVER LET GO 1-3
By **Robert Baptiste**

NEW TO THE GAME 1-3
MONEY, MURDER & MEMORIES 1-3
By **Malik D. Rice**

CREAM 2-3
THE STREETS WILL TALK
By **Yolanda Moore**

THE STREETS WILL NEVER CLOSE 1-3
By **K'ajji**

LIFE OF A SAVAGE 1-4
A GANGSTA'S QUR'AN 1-4
MURDA SEASON 1-3
GANGLAND CARTEL 1-3
CHI'RAQ GANGSTAS 1-4
KILLERS ON ELM STREET 1-3
JACK BOYZ N DA BRONX 1-3
A DOPEBOY'S DREAM 1-3
JACK BOYS VS DOPE BOYS 1-3
COKE GIRLZ
COKE BOYS
SOSA GANG 1&2
BRONX SAVAGES
BODYMORE KINGPINS
BLOOD OF A GOON
By **Romell Tukes**

CONCRETE KILLA 1-3
VICIOUS LOYALTY 1-3
By **Kingpen**

THE ULTIMATE SACRIFICE 1-6
KHADIFI
IF YOU CROSS ME ONCE 1-3
ANGEL 1-4
IN THE BLINK OF AN EYE
By **Anthony Fields**

THE LIFE OF A HOOD STAR
By **Ca$h & Rashia Wilson**

NIGHTMARES OF A HUSTLA 1-3
BLOOD AND GAMES 1&2
By **King Dream**

GHOST MOB
By **Stilloan Robinson**

HARD AND RUTHLESS 1&2
MOB TOWN 251
THE BILLIONAIRE BENTLEYS 1-3
REAL G'S MOVE IN SILENCE
By **Von Diesel**

MOB TIES 1-7
SOUL OF A HUSTLER, HEART OF A KILLER 1-3
GORILLAZ IN THE TRENCHES
By **SayNoMore**

BODYMORE MURDERLAND 1-3
THE BIRTH OF A GANGSTER 1-4
By **Delmont Player**

FOR THE LOVE OF A BOSS 1&2
By **C. D. Blue**

KILLA KOUNTY 1-5
By **Khufu**

MOBBED UP 1-4
THE BRICK MAN 1-5
THE COCAINE PRINCESS 1-10
STEPPERS 1-3
SUPER GREMLIN 1-4
By **King Rio**

MONEY GAME 1&2
By **Smoove Dolla**

A GANGSTA'S KARMA 1-4
By **FLAME**

KING OF THE TRENCHES 1-3
By **GHOST & TRANAY ADAMS**

QUEEN OF THE ZOO 1&2
By **Black Migo**

GRIMEY WAYS 1-3
BETRAYAL OF A G
By **Ray Vinci**

XMAS WITH AN ATL SHOOTER
By **Ca$h & Destiny Skai**

KING KILLA 1&2
By **Vincent "Vitto" Holloway**

BETRAYAL OF A THUG 1&2
By **Fre$h**

THE MURDER QUEENS 1-5
By **Michael Gallon**

FOR THE LOVE OF BLOOD 1-4
By **Jamel Mitchell**

HOOD CONSIGLIERE 1&2
NO TIME FOR ERROR
By **Keese**

PROTÉGÉ OF A LEGEND 1&2
LOVE IN THE TRENCHES 1&2
By **Corey Robinson**

THE PLUG'S RUTHLESS DAUGHTER
By **Tony Daniels**

BORN IN THE GRAVE 1-3
CRIME PAYS
By **Self Made Tay**

MOAN IN MY MOUTH
By **XTASY**

TORN BETWEEN A GANGSTER AND A GENTLEMAN
By **J-BLUNT & Miss Kim**

LOYALTY IS EVERYTHING 1-3
CITY OF SMOKE 1&2
By **Molotti**

HERE TODAY GONE TOMORROW 1&2
By **Fly Rock**

WOMEN LIE MEN LIE 1-4
FIFTY SHADES OF SNOW 1-3
STACK BEFORE YOU SPLURGE
GIRLS FALL LIKE DOMINOES
NAÏVE TO THE STREETS
By **ROY MILLIGAN**

PILLOW PRINCESS
By **S. Hawkins**

THE BUTTERFLY MAFIA 1-3
SALUTE MY SAVAGERY 1&2
By **Fumiya Payne**

THE LANE 1&2
By Ken-Ken Spence

THE PUSSY TRAP 1-5
By **Nene Capri**

DIRTY DNA
By **Blaque**

SANCTIFIED AND HORNY
by **XTASY**

BOOKS BY LDP'S CEO, CA$H

TRUST IN NO MAN
TRUST IN NO MAN 2
TRUST IN NO MAN 3
BONDED BY BLOOD
SHORTY GOT A THUG
THUGS CRY
THUGS CRY 2
THUGS CRY 3
TRUST NO BITCH
TRUST NO BITCH 2
TRUST NO BITCH 3
TIL MY CASKET DROPS
RESTRAINING ORDER
RESTRAINING ORDER 2
IN LOVE WITH A CONVICT
LIFE OF A HOOD STAR
XMAS WITH AN ATL SHOOTER